5F

OTHER TITLES
· FROM ·
SERPENT'S TAIL

MASKS

· THE ·
SIXTH
DAY

· THE ·
SIXTH
DAY

Andrée Chedid

Translated from the French by
Isobel Strachey

SERPENT'S
TAIL

BRITISH LIBRARY CATALOGUING IN PUBLICATION DATA

Chedid, Andrée
The sixth day
I. Title   II. Le sixième jour.   *English*
843'.914 [F]   PQ2637.1547
ISBN 1-85242-111-8

First published as Le sixième jour by René Julliard, Paris
Copyright © 1960 by René Julliard
First published in English by Anthony Blond
Translation © 1962 by Anthony Blond

This edition first published 1987 by
Serpent's Tail, 27 Montpelier Grove, London NW5

Printed in Great Britain by
WBC Print (Bristol) Ltd

· THE ·
SIXTH
DAY

PART I

"Listen . . . you may think it a story, but I tell you it's a fact. I'll tell you what I have to say as though it were the truth."

Plat. *Gorgias*.

CHAPTER 1

SHAKING its load of rubble, the cart jolted along the country road, with old Om* Hassan seated beside the driver.

" I'll put you down and clear off at once," he grumbled.

" As you like."

Her eyes were fixed on the horizon, waiting for her village to appear with the dawn. The man had tried several times to dissuade her from making the journey. " You're all right in Cairo; what do you want to go down there for? The cholera has been ravaging the countryside. It won't be a pretty sight for you."

" I must go."

The day before, she had explained her departure to her grandson Hassan, whom she was leaving for the first time.

" They're my people, little one, I must see them. I ought to have gone long ago, only it was impossible before; there were policemen about everywhere. Now we can go where we like. I shall only be away for one day. But I must go, don't you understand? "

He had nodded his head. He understood all right. She had only to speak to him in a certain way for him to know she meant to be understood. " Son of my

* Mother of Hassan.

dead daughter, son of my soul," she sighed, thinking about the child.

" How many years since you've been back to Barwat? " asked the carter.

" Seven years."

" Seven years, that's nothing. It's these last three months which count."

Dawn was breaking; the woman recognised her village at the bend of the road.

*

*   *

" I'm clearing off," the man told her, as soon as her feet had touched the ground.

Her face turned towards Barwat, Om Hassan heard the sound of the wheels disappearing and dying away behind her.

The houses, crushed under piles of branches and straw, could hardly be distinguished from the ground.

She walked a few steps, went up to the open doors. The interiors were dark, empty, full of charred objects. For fear of not hearing an answering voice, she dared not call out.

Presently the old woman returned and stood in the middle of the road. Some insurmountable force prevented her from going on. She crouched on the ground, took some of the earth in her hands, and pressed it to her cheek and mouth.

Someone called her:

" Why have you come here, Om Hassan? "

She rose up to the full height of her tall figure, and

walked slowly towards her nephew, who did not move from where he was standing by the water-tank. When she reached him she laid her hand on his shoulder with relief.

" You can go away again," continued Saleh, in a sullen voice. " You've arrived too late."

" Too late? "

" There are only the dead left here to welcome you."

The village was grey with the dawn. Clusters of mosquitoes criss-crossed over the surface of the tank, which was covered with a spongy yellow crust. Crows were flying low; she could hear the rustle of their wings.

" I left Cairo yesterday evening. I've been travelling all night."

" People in the towns don't get cholera. It's only for us."

" I've wanted to come for a long time."

" It's many years since you were one of us."

" Half of my heart remained with you."

She could not help thinking of Hassan as she looked at her nephew. Saleh wore a brown felt skullcap on his shaved head. She noticed his protruding cheek-bones, his sunken cheeks. The bottom of his indigo-blue tunic was dirty, his legs were covered in mud, his feet bare. Her grandson was always dressed in a clean tunic, with sandals on his feet. At Saleh's age he would be educated, and have a job in the town.

" You live too far away; you know nothing about us."

" No, I know nothing, Saleh."

" We've had eleven deaths in our family. As for the village, I've lost count. But the hospital is the worst! The ambulance arrived, the nurses forced their way into the houses, burnt our belongings, carried off the sick."

" Where to? "

" They never tell us."

" I found out in the end where they had taken my father and brother: under tents, right out in the desert. I've been there. At first they chased us away with sticks, my mother and me, but we returned shouting out the names of our people, so that they should know we hadn't deserted them, that we were there, near them. In the end I crept into one of the tents. It was horrible! The same face everywhere: blue, hollow, the tongue hanging out. The patients lie one beside the other on the sand, vomiting; two of them were already dead and left lying there. I called again, they all looked at me in a dazed way. A nurse came in wearing boots and a mask, he pushed me outside—before I could find my people. No one who hasn't lived through all this knows anything about it. Never shall I forget— Since then we've hidden our sick and even our dead! "

" I understand you, my son."

" Now it's finished. The ambulance comes, drives round, goes away again without anyone. Our mother fell ill a few days ago." Saleh added in a flat voice: " She died last night." Then he drew back, depriving the old woman of his support, and walked away without another word.

" I'm coming with you," she cried.

" Go back where you came from."

" No, we'll go along together."

He would never get over his resentment.

" Come along then," he said, shrugging his shoulders, " you only have to follow me."

*

*   *

They turned left, took a soot-coloured path. In the distance, on the waste land dotted with palm-trees, there were no children playing.

The path grew narrower. The houses, facing each other on either side, nearly touched their shoulders. A little boy with a round belly, running in the opposite direction, was caught up for a moment in the old woman's skirts. Disentangling himself, he pushed against her with his sticky little hands, and rushed off as fast as his legs would carry him.

" Where are all the people who used to live here? "

Without answering, Saleh took a turning to the left.

Om Hassan recognised the flat stone used by the old men as a seat. " If we had stayed here, this is where Saïd would have come to sit." She imagined him at dawn, sitting among the others, letting the beads of his rosary slip through his thumb and fore-finger.

The path wound past the building of unbaked bricks belonging to Hamar, the local constable, the only one-storeyed house in the whole village. The projecting platform which served as a balcony was collapsing, the wall round it was crumbling.

" It's all falling down here," said the woman.

" What's the use of a balcony to the dead? "

Farther on, he turned round.

" I came out to fetch this," he said, showing her the hoe he was carrying. " Otherwise you wouldn't have found me."

" I would have gone to your house."

" It isn't there any more."

" Have you moved? "

" They burnt our houses. Because of the cholera, the ambulance men came and set fire to them. And you, aren't you frightened? " he asked, putting his face close to hers.

" Come along," the woman cut him short. " Don't let's waste any time."

* * *

The sky was all at once whitewashed with light. There was not one finger's breadth of shadow left on its blue surface. " Sun which riseth all rosy over the rosy mountain," the old refrain came back to her mind, this time like the saddest of laments.

A buffalo, thin as a skeleton, dragging a rope, moved slowly out of a hovel, tilting its long head.

Soon afterwards, they came out into a tiny square where stood the common barn, the barber-chemist's shop, the grocery.

" They carried Taher off too. He never returned. They never come back."

" Don't think about these things any more."

" How can I stop thinking about them? They

won't get my mother. We're burying her tonight."

A piece of red cotton material, wedged between the shutters of the grocery, hung down to the ground. Flat cakes, a mixture of mud and straw, used as fuel in winter, were piled up against the wall of the barn. The rows of tin cans which served as pigeon-houses were empty of birds.

Farther on, Saleh showed her a strip of charred earth. " Look at that; whole families used to live there! "

She was seized with anguish and murmured: " Oh, God protect the child until I get back! "

" Where is the child? " asked Saleh, as though guessing her thoughts.

" I left him with the schoolmaster."

" And my uncle Saïd? "

" He can't move about any more. Yaccoub the carpenter looks after him when I'm not there."

" What was the good of leaving them? " His voice grated like a file. " They need you, and we don't! "

" You must forgive me if I can't do anything to help you. I couldn't bear not to share your troubles."

" Who can share another person's troubles? "

*
*   *

The path crawled out of the village, as far as the banks of a narrow canal. Near a tamarisk, top-heavy with the weight of its leaves, Saleh showed the old woman a cluster of huts built of maize stalks.

" There it is."

They both skirted an overturned plough which blocked the way. A little girl with her head covered in a jute sack ran out to meet them. Her face was grey and pinched, and below her frayed dress her legs were covered with sores.

" Quick, quick, before they come and take her away from us," she panted.

" This is Nefissa, one of your nieces," Saleh told the old woman.

" Did you find the hoe? " asked the child.

He showed it to her. Then they began to run; Om Hassan found it difficult to keep up with them. Outside the door, Saleh ordered the little girl to keep watch.

" They go on their rounds today. If you hear them, if you see them, knock three times."

" I know."

As Saddika crossed the threshold, a stale smell of wet pickling-brine filled her nostrils. Saleh explained to the three young men grouped in the centre of the room who this woman was. They turned round, briefly nodded their heads. She recognised Mustapha because of his wall eye. Omar the youngest; but not the third. Perhaps it was Rachid? But already, turning their backs on her, they had begun whispering again. A young woman with sunken pock-marked cheeks and eyebrows shaped like a swallow fanned herself with a corner of her veil; her chin on her bosom, she was staring mistrustfully at the old woman.

There was no furniture in the room, except, shoved away in a corner, one of those jars used for storing food. A bunch of large red onions hung from the ceiling.

The woman slowly advanced, looking for the body of her sister, and her nephews all withdrew in a bunch and watched her with unashamed curiosity while she confronted the corpse. The toes of her sandals touched the horny upturned naked feet.

Rolled up in her black clothes, lying on the ground itself, Salma appeared immeasurably long. Her narrow, tanned face reminded Saddika of a mummy, which she had seen with Hassan and the young schoolmaster in a museum, behind a dusty sheet of glass. That mask no longer had any resemblance to the blooming face of her younger sister. It seemed as though, under the skin, a net of dry and crinkled threads were holding the features in place.

For a moment Om Hassan pictured the Salma of the past: the village midwife with her hands on her sturdy hips, pealing with laughter. She looked again at the extended body, and the two images lay there side by side, as though in hallucination. The old woman closed her eyes.

" Go and sit down, aunt."

She found herself sitting down beside the young woman. The girl's face was so close to hers that Saddika could see in the pierced partition between her nostrils the circle of string which would one day be replaced by a gold ring.

" She received the last letter you had written* to her," shouted Saleh. " You said you were a washer-

* By a professional letter-writer.

woman, that you earned a good living, that you had a lot of clients and she ought to come and join you. But she would never have left us."

He let out a great laugh which reminded her of the dead woman's.

The men now began to move round the corpse, while on her still plump fingers the old woman counted those who were absent. Omar cut the red cord which hung round his mother's neck in order to detach the key of her dowry-box; its garish colours seemed out of place on this day of burial. They had to use the hoe to break a second lock. All together, they took out the contents. Soon a wide variety of objects strewed the ground—a cooking-pot, pieces of stuff, dried herbs, Turkish slippers, pepper, a sachet of kohl, needles, five gold bracelets, and even some eggs.

Suddenly they heard three knocks, and Nefissa rushed in, biting her nails and tugging with the other hand at the end of her reddish plait.

" We must do it quickly," said Saleh.

The four of them carried the body to the box, and then struggled to fit it inside. The corpse was adamant and much too long. They made several attempts before replacing it again on the ground.

" Hurry up, they're visiting the houses," murmured the child.

" Saw off her legs," someone suggested.

Om Hassan cried out and covered her face with her hands.

" What use are her legs to her? " the same voice insisted.

Saleh's face flamed with anger; he struck his brother with all his strength and sent him flying against the opposite wall.

Seeping through the branches, the sun's rays doubled the heat of the room. The men lifted up the corpse a second time, but however much they turned, raised, lowered it, bumping it each time against the lining of the box, there was nothing to be done.

The little girl was dancing up and down beside the half-open door. Soon they heard the sound of an engine starting up.

" We must hide her until this evening," whispered Saleh. " Let's go quickly into the fields."

The old woman, followed by the girl, drew near to help them.

*

* *

Bearing their heavy burden, the six of them passed by the well with its long pump-handle, the counter-weight entangled in weeds. On the other side of the stretch of water, just beyond the furze bushes, the country spread out as flat as the palm of your hand.

There was no one in sight. Not a single labourer. Not even a child perched on a buffalo, and no buffalo was turning round the wheel with its buckets.

The old woman, who was supporting the head of the corpse, could not take her eyes from the shrivelled face.

" We'll bury her tonight, when all is quiet," said Saleh.

Near the hut, the little girl was making signs to

them to hurry. They crossed the swaying footbridge. Below the chequered plantations, they took the path along the banks of the river and sank up to their ankles in the muddy soil. At last, coming to a huge clump of papyrus, they stooped to lay Salma on the ground. The corpse was heavy, it sank half-way up into the slime.

Om Hassan took off her necklace of yellow pearls and wound it round the cold blue fist.

Then each one returned by a different path.

CHAPTER 2

Om Hassan alighted from the grey lorry at one of the gates of the town.

She must change her expression and clear her mind of its buried impressions before she saw Hassan again. She took a deep breath, and crossing an open space continued on her way into her own quarter. Here the houses were crowded together, overhung by a minaret and by two palm trees roughly jostling in the wind.

She hurried into the first narrow street, with the idea of reaching her grandson as soon as possible.

Presently she was climbing over a pile of damp refuse buzzing with flies, and lifting up her skirts as she passed by the side of a greenish puddle into which children were throwing stones. Taher the albino turned round and stared at her with his pink eyes. He was fat and walked with a stagger.

Children with ebony-black eyes were running about everywhere. Abdalla pushed a bicycle wheel. Amin and Sami were quarrelling over an empty tin. Little girls in a motley of brightly coloured calico, with muslin handkerchiefs knotted at the four corners on their fuzzy hair, were making themselves dolls out of rags and bits of string.

"Dress me!" whimpered Yassim, tugging a piece of stuff away from them. He pulled a face, showing them his naked back. His ragged tunic was only held together by the sleeves. " My dress is as thin as a ' Konafa '* leaf, an offence to your eyes! " He went off into a huge peal of laughter, followed by the rest of them.

" Where have you been, Om Hassan? " asked Halima, recognising the old woman with difficulty through her purulent eyelids.

Dressed in red, she sat curled up, endlessly caressing a cat which she held imprisoned between her knees.

" I went on a journey."

" Ah! On a journey." Satisfied with this reply, she went on stroking the cat. " Biss, biss, my pretty one, my Blackie . . ."

Farther on the old woman had to push her way through a mob. Young Barsoum, dressed in striped pyjamas, perched on a wooden box, was miming the cholera. He had stuck patches of green paper on his forehead, his eyelids and his cheeks; his mouth was wide open, his hands pressed to his stomach, his eyes nearly rolled back into his head, as he parodied the pains and the agony of a patient.

" I've got cholera! Cholera! " he yelled above the applause.

" Where do you come from? " asked Ali the bedouin, from where he stood in front of his hut made of palm leaves and rags, with his sheep beside him as usual.

" I've no time for you. I haven't seen my grand-son for two days."

* Flake pastry.

His skin the colour of spice, his piercing glance, his narrow jaws and fine wrists distinguished him from the others.

" Don't go away like that," he said. " I want to say good-bye, because I shall be far away tomorrow."

" Where are you going ? "

" I couldn't get used to it. When there are too many people the air is bad. I can't breathe here. I'm going back to my desert."

" I don't know what you mean," she told him dryly.

He caught her by the arm.

" One minute more— Listen: ' When God created all things, he joined a second to each one of them. I'm going to Syria, said Reason; I'm going with you, said Rebellion. I'm going into the desert, said Misery; I'll go with you, said Health. Plenty said: I'm going into Egypt; I'll accompany you, said Resignation.' "

" I don't understand you. I couldn't live far away from all these people."

With a wide gesture she showed him the crowds coming and going through the intersecting lanes: the woman carrying her child pick-a-back on her shoulders, the dyer with his fingers stained blue, caught up in an argument; the sweet-potato-seller and the cucumber vendor each pushing his barrow and vainly trying to pass the other. She even looked tenderly at Zakieh of the scorpion's tongue and ferret's eyes, squatting on her mat scrutinising the passers-by. She showed him Amina the little tomato-seller and the blind man asleep beside the doorway of the barber's shop.

" I couldn't live without them."

" You're the one who doesn't understand, woman! "

" You're wasting my time, Ali. I've already told you the child is waiting for me."

She left him abruptly without saying good-bye and threaded her way through the crowd, bending her head to avoid being recognised again. But just as she was about to enter the lane of the little cakes, she was seized with remorse and turned back to see if she could see the bedouin. In vain. Then she raised her arm above her head, and waved her hand high over the sea of heads, and forced a shout:

" May good health attend you, Ali! "

The reply came at once:

" Good health be with you, Om Hassan! "

*
* *

The school consisted of one long room coated with ochre-yellow plaster, and although it was fairly new, the walls had already begun to crack. An open space used as a market place separated it from the other dwellings.

Om Hassan went to sit on one of the three steps, and gently pushed open the door to look inside the classroom. There were only about thirty pupils, and her heart beat faster when she saw in the first row the sharply outlined nape of Hassan's neck and his big, sticking-out ears.

On the tiny dais, the young master was finishing his writing on the blackboard. He wore a red cap, a suit of European style, and was dressed up in spite of the heat in a worn, olive-coloured overcoat which fitted badly and hampered his movements. When he turned round Saddika nodded her head as if to demonstrate her complete approval. Everything about this young man inspired her with confidence. She thought his face with its finely modelled features handsome, his gaze full of light, and " his smile ", she said, " refreshes like the dew ". But when the *oustaz* Selim wished to explain his opinions with regard to ignorance, poverty and injustice, his appearance was suddenly transformed. His ears burned hotly and the veins stood out on his forehead. A multitude of ideas jostled each other in his head and a strange violence possessed him. Words stumbled out of his mouth, his sentences became confused; floods of generosity and rebelliousness, of which he was barely conscious, assailed him, before he was in a position either to understand or direct them.

When he was teaching, however, his voice was in contrast melodious and crystalline; every word shone like a pebble taken out of the water.

" The class is finished; you may get up, children," he said, clapping his hands.

Hassan disappeared behind a mass of backs; even when she stretched out her neck Saddika could no longer catch sight of him.

" We will end by repeating the hygiene lesson. Do you know it by heart ? "

" Yes."

" Then all together: Why have you a nose? " he asked them.

" In order to breathe," replied the pupils.

The old woman knew all the answers and joined her voice with theirs:

" In order to breathe— "

" Why must you breathe? "

" In order to live."

" And if your nose were blocked up? "

" I would die."

" Is fresh air a good thing? "

" Yes."

" Have you any windows at home? "

" Yes! " shouted most of them.

" So then if fresh air is a good thing and if there are windows in your house, what ought you to do? "

" Open them! "

" Open them," repeated Om Hassan.

" Well done, children! Very well said. You may go now."

They rushed towards the entrance and the old woman moved down to the bottom of the steps to let them stream past.

Hassan was the last to appear. He threw himself into her arms.

* *
* *

Saddika dreamed of returning to those laundry rooms situated on roof-gardens high up in the sky, and of taking Hassan there again as she used to do. There, seated in front of a huge metal wash-basin, her arms plunged up to the elbows in the soapy water, she used to wash the linen and the child played round her. Or leaning over the parapet in that wealthy quarter, he watched the world below. The Nile glittered between gaudy lights; the great houses seated on stone foundations, decked out with colonnaded balconies and flights of marble steps, were rooted in an eternity of time. The lawns of the gardens and the flowers were like ceremonial carpets.

In the evening, like two pilgrims, they would leave one world for another, and hand in hand affectionately rediscover a dusty path, flimsy houses and also a dearth of flowers.

Only Saïd complained sometimes as though the earth still clung to his heart. " Everything's kinder in the country," he sighed. " There's shade under every tree and each tree is a bit like your house." A recurring nightmare obsessed him: he was lying, bound hand and foot on the macadam while the burning sun drilled a hole through his breast.

Om Hassan was a changed woman after her return from Barwat. She believed the heavens were about to fall. In spite of Hassan's fresh skin, his large, lively black eyes, his sturdy body and firm legs, the sight of him tormented her with anxiety.

*
* *

One morning when Saddika arrived at the school she

found only Hassan left talking to the young school-master at the end of the room. He came forward followed by the child.

Half-way across the classroom, the *oustaz* Selim seemed to lose his balance, then he went on walk-ing, dragging his legs and supporting himself on the desks.

" What's the matter with you? " Om Hassan called to him from the doorway.

He took a few more steps and just managed to reach the door, the child anxiously holding him up with his little arms. Out of breath, suddenly gripping his stomach, the young master leant back against the open door.

" What is it? "

The little square was empty, riddled by the rays of the midday sun. The young man's lips moved but no sound came out of his mouth. Suddenly he drew a large blackish-brown handkerchief out of his pocket, and turning his back began to vomit.

" Hassan, run and fetch the ambulance," he gasped at last.

" The ambulance? What for? " asked the old woman.

" He must go at once—"

" But what is wrong with you?" she persisted.

" It's the cholera. I know it is."

" You're wrong. There's no more cholera."

" Don't argue woman, I know what I'm saying—"
He looked at her with an exhausted face and entreated her:

" Let the child go."

" It's madness. If they take you, we'll never see you again." She remembered Saleh's description. " If you only knew what happens there."

" I'm an educated man," he said. Then his head fell forward: " An educated man must go to hospital. As an example—"

His arms hung down at his sides, his legs trembled; he forced himself none the less to preserve an attitude of dignity and with what was left of his voice he insisted:

" Hassan, your teacher commands you to go and fetch the ambulance."

Hassan raised his eyes and looked at his grandmother.

" There are no more ambulances," she retorted. " They haven't been near us for weeks. The cholera is dead."

" I recognise the symptoms. I've read about it in books, woman; you don't understand."

" Very well," she admitted. " It is the cholera. But if so, we'll look after you, I and the child. No one will know anything about it. Lean on my shoulder and I'll take you to your house."

" You are mad, mad—" Each word was costing him a considerable effort. " Do you know that your ignorance can be the cause of great misfortunes?"

What other misfortune was there at that moment than that of letting him go?

" By yourself, alone . . . You'll be alone!" she wailed.

"Run as far as the main street," he said to the child. "There you must ask the first policeman. He'll know what to do."

The child rushed down the three steps, crossed the square and was gone.

"Keep a careful watch over your grandson; we have been too much together these last few days." He was expressing himself better, the illness was giving him a respite: "Please stand on the top step, woman, well in front of me to hide me from the passers-by. It will be better if no one in the district hears of this until after I have left."

She did as he told her.

"I felt as though I had a fire in my entrails just then." He took a box of cigarettes out of his pocket and tried to lift one to his lips, but soon gave it up. "In six days I shall be cured. Don't forget what I tell you. On the sixth day either one dies or one recovers. On the sixth day—" he added, remembering the words used in the newspaper—"there is a ve-ri-ta-ble re-sur-rec-tion!" Then with a faint smile: "Don't be upset. Six days are soon over, and I shall be back there again."

He made a vague gesture with his arm towards the end of the classroom.

*

* *

White and glistening like a thousand spears in the sun, the ambulance burst into the square, with Hassan clinging to the footboard, and pulled up in the middle of it, raising a cloud of dust.

Three men in overalls alighted. Without asking questions, they pushed Om Hassan to one side and prepared to take hold of the patient.

" Where are you taking him?"

Nobody answered her. Placing their arms under the young man's armpits, they dragged him off. She clung to one of the nurses' sleeves.

" He's a relative of mine. I'll have to visit him."

" There's no visiting. Keep away and let us get on with our work."

" I want to know. He is by himself. I can't leave him all alone."

" That's enough," said the man, freeing himself from her grasp. " It's the same for everyone. You're wasting our time."

The young master was panting in the sun as though his heart would break.

" Let them alone. I'll come back on the sixth day. Please don't interfere; let them alone," he besought her, giving himself up to the nurses' hands, and relieved not to have to make any further effort.

In a few seconds they had carried him into the ambulance and laid him on a stretcher. Saddika stood quite still, her legs like stone, her tongue like lead. But the moment the car started to move, she ran forward, cupping her hands round her mouth like a trumpet and yelled into the black cage:

" You'll come back! You'll certainly come back. We'll be there, Hassan and I, on the sixth—"

The door banged shut, cutting her sentence short. " The sixth day," she finished in a low voice.

*

* *

On the sixth day Hassan and the old woman, seated side by side on the bottom step of the deserted school, waited until the middle of the night. No one came.

" We'll go home," said Om Hassan.

They walked slowly away along the path reddened by the moon, often turning to look back.

When they reached their house, the child snatched up a stone with a furious gesture, and sent it hurtling off as far as he could.

The door creaked open.

" Ah, there you are at last! " exclaimed Saïd, in his whining voice. " Is this the way you leave a poor old man all alone? "

The woman and child waited patiently for six more days. But their vigil was always in vain.

Then without admitting it, they both gave up hope.

THE days followed each other sadly. Because of a few isolated cases there was talk of a second bout of cholera. The crowded districts were again frequently visited, and the siren of the ambulance haunted them obsessively once more. Because of all these precautions, the old woman had not been able to begin work again. As for the child, deprived of school, he wandered about all over the place between his meals. Om Hassan lost sight of him for days together. He slipped through the interlacing alleys like a cat.

One morning there were huge brownish stains round his eyes. But the moment Saddika turned away to look after the old man, Hassan ran out of the house and escaped from her. She spent the morning waiting for him to return. She remembered that the evening before he had pushed away Fifo the nanny-goat, instead of climbing on to her back as usual; then he had eaten little, and slept badly, tossing in his sleep. She thought of it all the morning.

When it was his usual hour to come home there was no sign of him; she began to walk up and down the room without speaking a word.

Stretched out on a mat, his paralysed legs rolled up in a sack, his body hidden under a cotton coverlet, Saïd followed her with his eyes. Only the old man's face and hands were visible, a face covered with wrinkles, and on either side of his felt cap his ears with drooping lobes.

All the winds of the desert were rustling in his wife's clothes! She came and went, lost in her veils.

Enough, enough—

The man had a taciturn disposition. He did not like either the movement or the noise, and closed his eyes in order not to take it in any more.

But through his closed eyelids he still felt that large shadow pass and re-pass, persistently crossing the short space between one wall and the other.

Presently he turned his head slightly to the right, trying to catch a glimpse of the entrance; the door was made of wooden planks hastily nailed together and fastened on the outside after the child had gone out, it had shut out the street, and the sight of it plunged him into a deep sadness. Then he gazed into the tiny yard in the opposite corner, and saw Fifo the nanny-goat tied to the wheel of the cart which they had used for their removal. Bound to her rope, Fifo let her greenish tongue hang out. "Err, err—" murmured Saïd, with a soft inflexion to attract the animal's attention. For a moment the man and the beast looked into each other's eyes; then the man sighed and turned his head away again.

Suddenly interrupting her pacing, the old woman leant up against the door, pushed it towards the outside with both hands, and went out. A ray of light pierced the room. With her body bent forward and neck outstretched, she searched for the child. She advanced a few steps and started down the first alley, only to leave it and turn down another. But she very soon gave up searching them all, preferring to station herself in front of her hovel, and keep watch in several directions at once. She was also fearful of arousing the curiosity of the neighbours. Each case tracked down received a reward, and perhaps someone might betray her for love of money.

For the first time in her life she was full of mistrust; everyone looked to her like a possible informer. Seated on her wooden box, Zakieh the grandmother, twisted like a root, was uglier than age itself; she was sure to be watching Om Hassan's every movement with her lynx's eyes. The dyer with his blue fingers passed by in front of her with a studied slowness which appalled her. Little Amina pretended to weigh tomatoes on a pair of scales, bigger than herself; in reality she was observing everything between half-closed eyelids.

Om Hassan returned to the room and paced it again.

" Stop, for pity's sake," Saïd besought her " you're rocking the room! For pity's sake—" His sentence became incomprehensible. Sometimes his tongue became involved in a muddle of words and nothing would pass clearly through his lips. But his wife always understood him. Except today. Today she seemed to be struck deaf.

However, a few seconds later, a distant sound held her motionless.

The siren was shrieking again. Nearer this time.

The woman went out to stand in the doorway, stretching herself to look out; she was a dark mass blocking out the daylight, plunging the interior of the room into an inky blackness. Saïd had the impression that he was falling to the bottom of a well. He joined his hands together to beg for a word, a gesture, no matter what. But Saddika was miles away from the room.

" Don't you see him yet? " he breathed, making an effort to share his wife's anguish.

She did not answer. She could only hear the rumble of the motor car and the blood pulsing inside her temples; her heart was in her mouth.

Midday. The sun beat down cruelly. The ambulance drove away into the distance, as she guessed from the sound of the wheels.

" Don't you see him yet? "

Saïd's voice broke through and Om Hassan turned round and fixed the old man with her grey eyes. What was the use of adding to her anxiety?

" It's nothing. He won't be long. You can rest."

How wretched he looked. There was nothing left of his face but the bones, his fingers reminded her of willow-wands whitened in the sun. Had the past ever existed? Had this man ever stood erect? Given her orders? And she, always a few paces behind him? " If either of the two have to die, rather let it be the old man."

In order to make up for this sinister thought she fell on her knees at the foot of the mattress. Then taking a large red handkerchief from her pocket, she sponged her husband's face. Then she fanned

him, tilting the scarlet square backwards and forwards.

The man recovered his indifference and slowly
dropped off to sleep.

*

*   *

The ambulance drew up, this time a few yards off.
Saddika heard the metallic sound of the door slam-
ming, then footsteps. Soon afterwards—she had
not had time to get up—two nurses and a young girl
crossed the threshold, and surrounded the old man.

" Has he been vaccinated? What is he doing
lying on the ground? Has he vomited? Is he cold?
Any dizziness? Diarrhoea? "

The nurses, dressed in white overalls buttoned
at the back and reaching to their ankles, with little
white linen caps on their heads, bent over the old
man and continued to pester him. The young girl
looked round her—it was her first visit to this district. The acrid smell of the room had disagreeably
surprised her ever since she entered it, and she
coughed into her hand, with her face turned to the
wall.

Exasperated by the number and rapidity of the
questions, Saddika drew herself up:

" Don't you see he is paralysed? He hasn't got
the cholera. He is paralysed! Paralysed—do you
understand? "

The first nurse went down on one knee, ceremoniously took off his spectacles, breathed on them
and rubbed them with a corner of his overall,

before replacing them on his nose. Even with these glasses he saw badly, and in examining the old man he seemed to be sniffing at him.

" There's nothing wrong with him. We were misinformed," he concluded.

The second nurse nodded his head in agreement. The young girl made a note in her little black notebook: " Nothing to report."

" We can go," the first nurse then remarked.

The other one always followed him. He waddled like a duck and stretched up his neck to give himself height. In spite of her flat heels the young girl was the tallest of the three; her long hair held back by a hairnet gave her an air of severity.

" Are there only you two here? " the second nurse suddenly asked, just as he was crossing the threshold.

" There are only the two of us," lied the woman.

The epidemic was reaching its end; the chief nurse decided to drop the would-be investigation. A bad joker had pointed out this alley. So much the worse— At this hour the sun ordered one to rest. The nurse was hungry and thirsty. He looked forward with delight to his approaching siesta. In his half-dream, Khadria the daughter of the café proprietor, with her breasts bursting through her pink bodice, and the fleshy white palms of her hands, came ever closer to him, smiling. Soon he would ask her father if he could marry her. " I am an official," he would say to Mustapha. It would be an honour to have him for a son-in-law.

The young girl had not followed them. She

wanted to speak to the old woman alone: but the other cut short all her advances. If she had dared, Om Hassan would have thrown the intruder out. What reason had she for persisting like this, proposing help, lavishing advice?

" Don't eat anything raw. You must wash yourself to protect you from the cholera. . . . Boil everything, be careful to . . ." Her voice buzzed like a wasp. Going to the only shelf she drew her attention to the oil stove. " You must use it." Next she examined the copper casserole: " It's clean," she said approvingly.

" I am a washerwoman," retorted the old woman. Then she pointed to the round-bellied pitcher:

" Where do you fetch your water? "

" From the pump."

" That's a good thing, but I repeat, you must boil it as well."

" Yes, yes . . . yes . . . yes . . ."

Saddika would have showered her with " yeses," crowned her with " yes," if only she would have gone away.

" I would like to come and help you. Now, or later on, whenever you like," she stammered. In spite of her scarcely rouged lips, her pale cheeks, her hair-style, her deliberately dull clothes, she belonged to another world. A piece of looking-glass fixed to the wall, captured their two faces together for a moment. The old woman noticed the reflection with a shock and all at once remembered Saleh's phrase: " You have never been one of us . . ."

" My name is Dana—Dana S—— I'll come back,"
she insisted, and tearing a leaf out of her notebook
she wrote down her address. " If one day you should
need me, this is where you can find me."

" Thank you," murmured the woman, thrusting
the paper into her bodice and going to the door
which she pushed open.

But the young girl did not budge. Her gaze
moved slowly round the room, settling on the low
ceiling, the black walls, the mats on the floor, the
line hanging between two nails which also served
as a wardrobe. She shook her head sadly, unable to
resign herself to leaving. The old woman already
imagined she heard the " Forgive me," which she
would doubtless add in her embarrassed way.

" Good-bye," said Saddika, at the end of her
patience.

Finally the girl walked towards the entrance, but
with regret, lingering still in front of the door.

" Au revoir," she said at last.

*

* *

As soon as she heard the car drive away, Saddika
prostrated herself and kissed the ground several
times before resuming her watch.

There was no one else but her about. It was the
hour when the sun was let loose and everyone took
cover. She did not have long to wait.

A slender, irresolute figure came in sight at the
end of an alley.

The woman hesitated. She recognised the blue

tunic but it was not fluttering and flapping round firm calves and bounding legs. The blue tunic clung to him, impeding his steps. The child reeled, his body bent double, his hands pressed against his belly.

" Hassan! "

At once, lifting up her skirts, she began running towards him.

Moaning, he threw himself into her arms. At first she pressed him to her bosom without questioning him. Then, getting up, she tried to take him along with her as quickly as possible. He struggled at first not to let her carry him. She clamped her hand over the child's mouth to stifle his groans, and with the other arm encircling his waist she dragged him towards her open door. Hassan's heels raked the path, raising clouds of dust.

At last, having crossed the threshold, Saddika violently banged the door and pushed the bolt across it.

CHAPTER 4

EXCEPT for that screw which had fallen off weeks ago and was buried somewhere in the flattened earth, the bolt held firmly. The rough bar, thrust as far as it would go into the catch, gave the door a robust air in spite of its frailty. The woman heaved a sigh of relief. She felt safe behind those planks barred with iron, solidly protected from the neighbours, the sun and the street.

Still dragging Hassan, she brought him to the end of the room, as far as possible from the old man.

Standing the child in front of the tiny window, she crouched before him, panting, hardly daring to look at him. Then with both hands she began to feel over his whole body. Through the blue material, his heart beat as usual, the shape of his stomach was the same, with that slight rounding towards the base. She lifted the tunic. The skin was warm, scarcely grained on the hips; they were the same smooth thighs, the same rough knees. Her fingers gradually reassured her. She no longer trembled.

Turning her face towards the yellow rays which penetrated the window-pane, she allowed herself a few seconds respite. Then she raised her arms again. This time she took the child by the shoulders. She held him thus for a long time, as if her hands could communicate strength to Hassan, and a certain peace.

Still lying on his back, the old man was gasping; he felt as if his chest were weighted with a stone which ceaselessly grew larger. Usually everything became easier after the child's return. His shadow moving about and his voice gave life to the walls. Saïd knew that Hassan had come in, but today, the heaviness, the darkness persisted. A deadly presentiment seized him, he could not prevent himself from letting out a raucous cry.

"Be quiet," entreated the woman. "I can't attend to you just now."

After this yell, the old man felt relieved. Thrusting the woman and child out of his mind, he buried himself, lost himself once more in the interior of his body.

Disturbed by the man's crying out, Saddika shuddered and her hands let go of Hassan's shoulders. How was it she had failed to notice that the child's pupils were fixed and the whites of his eyes had lost all their transparency? And his ears? Hassan's large, sticking-out ears, always so attentive to what was going on farther away, were stunted and flattened, their skin all blistered. His mouth was almost without lips, his dimples had disappeared.

The old woman slewed round and drew back a little to contemplate the child from head to foot. His twisted body reminded her of those pieces of still grey linen which she squeezed out after the first soaping. This boy who used to leap about the quarter as though he were held to the sky by an invisible thread was now rooted to the ground!

" Do you feel ill, my son? "

At once she regretted her question:

" Oh well, it's nothing. It'll pass. . . . It won't be anything."

Hassan's only answer was to take a few steps forward and then throw himself with all his weight against his grandmother. He unloaded himself on to her. He could no longer bear, no longer even share the burden of his own life. His body all of a sudden weighed as much as those of a thousand children put together.

With her free hand the woman took off the child's cotton cap and lightly ruffled his scalp. Hassan's hair had grown too much. " I will take him to the barber; if not, he'll have lice." She stroked the little tuft, bushy and thick, growing on the front of his head, and let herself be distracted by everything which made the child seem like the Hassan of other days.

But suddenly he pushed her away and jumped back with both hands plastered against his stomach, making a horrible grimace. He had lifted up his clothes, uncovering his legs, his thighs and the lower part of his belly. A fetid stench spread through the room. The woman quickly pulled the large red handkerchief out of her pocket, and hastened to clean all the dirt off the child's body.

" It's nothing, it's nothing. I swear it."

On her knees she dabbed at his calves, his feet; and sponged the place where he was standing.

The old man came to his senses intermittently. But each of his returns was accompanied by such disturbances that he could only wish to avoid them, to withdraw from those who troubled his tranquillity. Something unusual and grave hovered round him, but he did not want to dwell on this thought: "Tomorrow . . . Tomorrow, we'll see . . ." And with a regular movement he swung his cupped hand to and fro beside the edge of his couch as though he were on a raft striving to get away from the banks of a stream by scooping the water.

The woman no longer tried to lie to herself. She had sat the child with his back against an empty box, and was preparing to wash the dirty clothes. Her store of water was used up; she tried the earthenware jar, there was scarcely enough to fill a cup. "I'll go to the pump later on." The most important thing was to remember the symptoms of the disease. It all came back to her. Certain arguments, scraps of sentences she had heard on the radio in the café, the dyer reading aloud from his newspaper. "Diarrhoea. Excretions with the appearance of rice water. Vomiting. Thirst. Drink, you must drink. The limbs become freezing cold, the skin is moist and the colour of melted wax."

There was no longer any doubt, the child had caught the disease. She said: " He has the cholera." She repeated it several times in order to convince herself. Then she repeated it without words, persuading herself that there was no other alternative than to accept the fact. That only by accepting it would she be able to fight and then overcome it.

How? She did not know yet, but she would think of a way. " On the sixth day, there is a ve-ri-ta-ble re-sur-rec-tion," the master had said. It would be true for Hassan. Effortlessly, she projected the child's image far away in front of her into the future. She saw him as an adolescent, standing up and walking with an assured step. She saw Hassan in one place and the cholera in another. At present Hassan and the cholera were one. They had to be taken together. One with the other. Death with life. One could no longer separate anything. One had to get through that. Then all would be well.

Bending over the child, whose head fell heavily first to one side and then the other, Saddika supported it between her two hands, her fingers interlacing behind the nape of Hassan's neck.

Delivered from his cramping pains, from the sensation of not being able to contain himself, from the stickiness which had covered his legs, he relaxed. The woman's warm hands pressed against his ears, gave rise to the noise of beating wings, of evening breezes, of drums.

The child was reminded of the huge shell with crinkled edges and orange-coloured centre that the cigarette-seller had brought from Alexandria. Barsoum was the only one in the district who had seen the sea.

" Hold it— Listen— " he often said to Hassan. Merely to possess such an object gave him authority and prestige.

That sound which the child sometimes liked to recapture in the evening before going to sleep, by pushing his forefingers into his ears—he heard it now:

" The sea! " he whispered.

" Yes, the sea! " repeated the old woman.

In order to prolong his pleasure, Saddika kept her arms outstretched until they were completely numb.

When she removed them, his head stayed upright. With a roguish air, Hassan moistened his bottom lip with the tip of his tongue. Then he stood up, apparently without any difficulty. He was steady on his legs. He separated them a little to hold himself even better. Thrusting his hand into his pocket, he took out a spongy green ball which seemed to have been moth-eaten in places. His fingers could not hold it and it slid down, bounced feebly on the ground and lodged against the edge of the mattress. The old man recognised it at a touch and seized hold of it.

The ball was soft, pliable. Saïd began to knead it. Sleep carpeted the ceiling, the walls, the room became wadded and grew smaller and smaller: a cage, a sentry-box, a coffin. Inside the shelter of this coffin the old man could forget everything. The ball was woolly, soft to the fingers. So soft, like a presence. Sleep was a round, a prayer, a well . . .

*
* *

" Everything is going round," wailed the child.

He tottered, clutching at the old woman. This time she sat down, laying the child across her knees. His nostrils became pinched, his lips turned blue. His lively coal-black eyes seemed now to be made of some flabby, tarnished substance. Hassan stirred restlessly. She rocked him. He was still restless. In order to soothe him and give herself time to think she began talking to him out loud, telling stories as she always did.

"We'll go to the river tomorrow. I'll stick a reed into my old shoe, it will become a boat and we can get into it. . . . We'll take a goose, a hen, a dog and Fifo the goat. For every boat floating on the water there are a hundred underneath it."

She told him everything which came into her head and the child listened:

"The moustaches of the public letter-writer are made of grass. The letters he traces are as delicate as eyelids. When you are big your letters will be like stars, like avenues, like cities . . ." The child grew quiet. One day he would grow up. That was certain. "The shade, the night, are the sun's masks. . . . Do you understand me, little one? The sun has no companion. He plays alone. He's always there, behind his dark faces. He hides himself but he never dies. He always comes back. . . . Illness is the same. You know what illness is?" She waited a moment for the words to come. ". . . It too is a mask. A great net in which one is caught, as fish are caught. But there are always fish which fight and escape. And then they are stronger than they ever were. . . . Fish in the bottom of a boat, they look like a silver carpet! But under the water there are fish which resist the monsters and live, that's the finest thing of all!"

The child lay quiet. The day waned; the light from the skylight became dim.

"Who knows, little one, if one dug a hole down into the earth's belly, perhaps one might find living stones? Yes, perhaps the stones are full of life and crackle? Everything is crackling. The pains, the tears of this world are probably eternally crackling in the heart of God."

Hassan dropped off to sleep. It was as if a bucket of sand were being emptied into the old woman's temples; her words became confused:

"When the storks next fly over, we will go and watch them from the top of the citadel. . . . The storks . . ."

Her head fell forward, heavy as lead, dragging her neck down.

How long had it lasted?

*
* *

Suddenly the ambulance was projected, throbbing, into the room. Enormous. Harshly white. The woman was blinded. Drawn up to her full height, she struggled against its iron muzzle. Around her the ceiling, the walls fell in.

"Get out of here! The child is mine— No one shall take him. No one!" she howled.

Her own cries, waking her up with a start, awoke the sleeping child.

CHAPTER 5

THERE was not a moment to lose.

Although she felt the child's weight on her legs, Saddika could not see Hassan. She lifted him up carefully, then bent forward and laid him down on the ground. Feeling her way in the darkness, she searched for an old iron box she kept in a corner of the room, containing some candles. She took one out, lit it and fixed it to the ground with a little melted wax. The room became translucent, she thought she saw eyes spying on her everywhere. The bolt with its missing screw seemed to her all amiss, a pretence. The door? An old man's fist could have forced it open.

" We'll go away," she said, bending over the child.

Hassan's eyes, immeasurably enlarged, were fixed on an invisible point. Suddenly, shaken by spasms, he raised himself up and vomited in floods. The old woman propped his back up against an overturned chair and wiped his mouth and the front of his tunic.

" I'm thirsty— "

His tongue hung out, dry and red at the edges.

" Wait, I'm coming back."

She half filled the tin cup and brought it to him. He dipped his lips into it, swallowed one or two mouthfuls and then soon brought them up again.

" Not the hospital," he entreated.

" Never! We're going away. Don't be afraid. Neither men nor death will catch up with us. The darkness is the disease of the sun, and remember the sun always overcomes it. You, you are my sun. You are my life. You can't die. Life can't die." She added: " I'm going to get the cart ready. Don't worry, we shall soon be far away."

With her candle in her hand, she entered the little yard. The goat came up to her, rubbing itself against her legs. She untied its rope. " Good Fifo," she said, " beautiful Fifo." Then while she examined the cart, she wondered where to go. A vision of trees, of water and green fields danced before her eyes. " I had better go into the centre of the town; no one will look for me there."

In the yellow glimmer, she examined the rails, pulled at the shafts, tapped the wheels. Everything appeared to be in order. She threw a bag of beans into the back of the cart, some loaves of maize, some preserved dates and a great many rags on which she would lay the child.

When she returned to the room she saw that the old man was still asleep. She knelt down beside him, and slipping her hand under the mattress drew out a purse made of goatskin, full of their savings. Then she counted the money and pocketed half before replacing the rest.

For a moment she was tempted to wake Saïd to explain their departure; then she thought it better to leave him to sleep. He would very quickly resign himself to their absence; it was a long time now since he had given up any kind of conflict. She told herself also that their neighbour Yaccoub would take care of him once more.

The child had allowed her to carry him into the little yard, and now lay helpless at the bottom of the cart.

" Where are we going ? " he anxiously asked.

" To get you well."

" Will it be far ? "

" It's just ahead of us."

Bending over him with the hot wax running down her fingers, she asked him not to cry, not to call out and to be patient. He whispered " Yes ", scarcely parting his lips. The faintly luminous rays lit up his mouth, disclosing the gap between his front teeth. Remembering that this was a sign of luck, the old woman placed the tip of her forefinger for an instant on the little space: " It is written," she said; " the sun is at the end of our journey."

Holding her candle, which she had fixed on to a fragment of pottery, she went back into the room for a last look round. The wick was nearly finished. Under the rosy glow of the flame the sleeping face of Saïd resembled a pewter mask.

" May God take you by the hand," she murmured, before going out.

Back again in the yard, the woman went towards the entrance. She lifted the latch of an old door which opened on to a tiny lane. She looked about her for some time, and finding it quiet, empty and sufficiently lit by the moon, she considered the moment had come to blow out her candle.

Then she began pushing the cart, forcing it, after several attempts, to pass over the stone on the threshold. Something moved behind her. Fifo, trailing her long rope, had followed them into the middle of the path. The woman shoved her away with a blow. The goat refused to go. " Kht—Kht— " she repeated, to drive her away, but without effect. Saddika then seized her by the horns and dragged her into the yard. Shutting the door on her, she barricaded it with an old boundary stone which she often used to tie up the animal outside.

Om Hassan set off again, her arms behind her, her body braced, pulling the cart and the child. But the goat kept on butting with her forehead against the closed door. For a long way the woman continued to hear the dull, reiterated thudding.

*

* *

The creaking wheels gnawed into the silence as she went and the old woman was afraid of waking the neighbours. She looked round several times but no door opened. " They are all with me," she said. " Even Zakieh, the grandmother, with her scorpion's tongue." Perhaps in their sluggish hearts they only meant to help her. This thought encouraged her until she came to the end of the closely built-up poorer district.

After a few more turnings, she came to the banks of the Nile. A long embankment road led to a bridge. The road was still under construction and stretched ahead for several kilometres. The woman hoped to get into the city before dawn. " A laundry-room would be a good refuge. But which one? "

The freshly asphalted surface of the road stuck to her thin soles. In its immobility, the enormous steam-roller seemed like a monster ready to crush her with its black cylinders. She passed it quickly. Close by on a mound of gravel a man dressed in unbleached linen lay full length, asleep. The noise of the wheels woke him with a start. He sat up, rubbing his eyes:

" Ho! Ho! " he cried, while the woman continued on her way. " Where are you going at this hour? You won't find a soul in the market."

" Go to sleep, man of God," she replied. " The night is made for sleeping."

As she spoke, Saddika slowly turned the cart round, so as to have it in front of her.

" You're right, old woman! The night is made for sleeping."

The workman lay down again, crossing his arms, but now the sharp stones bruised his back. " Accursed old woman, when I was sleeping so well." With so much tar about everywhere, he couldn't even let himself slide down on to the road-way. He sat up again. " She's going to do them all out of their sleep—accursed old woman! " he grumbled, watching her receding into the distance.

She did not meet anyone else the whole way along the embankment. Drops of sweat glistened on her forehead, her skirts were plastered against her moist legs. As soon as she had crossed the bridge, she rested for a moment against the parapet.

The child must have been asleep because nothing

was stirring inside the cart. Om Hassan closed her
eyes, breathed in a gust of air, blew it out, breathed
in again. Then before she ventured into the town,
she contemplated it for some time.

Under the tawny moon all its colours were
hardened. The city appeared hostile, cast in metal.
A number of crows, in a row on the edge of a
pavement, looked as if made of wrought iron. The
branches, the leaves of the few bushes seemed as
solid as lead. What was this town, with its brassy
sky, its cast-iron buildings, its etched trees, its
houses all in ridges, imprisoning motionless men?
Perhaps it was a dragon seized in a trance which
would rouse itself to destroy her and the child?

But what other way of escape was there? She
had no choice.

" We are nearly there," she said, loud enough for
Hassan to hear.

CHAPTER 6

THE streets stretched ahead between extinguished lamp-posts. In the distance Om Hassan caught sight of the municipal water-cart starting on its round. " The day will soon begin," she thought, pushing the cart more vigorously.

In the centre of the roundabout, the man of bronze stood on his pedestal, his large hand out-stretched as though questioning the city, where for a long time now he had had no place. Saddika passed round the statue and crossed the great avenue.

Most of the shop-fronts were masked by iron shutters, others could be seen through plate-glass laced with grating. A huge café famous for the quality of the broad-beans served there kept its doors half open all night, and one could see, far inside, the glimmer of a lighted room.

The town was waking up. Om Hassan believed they ought to hide as soon as possible.

She suddenly remembered the block of flats belonging to the Greek, at the end of a cul-de-sac; it was the nearest refuge. Madame Naïla, the dress-maker for whom Saddika had worked, owned a laundry-room there on the sixth floor. " I will ring her bell." She could see herself pressing in imagina-tion the well-polished brass knob with the tip of her forefinger. Already she seemed to hear tap-tapping along an interminable passage, the dressmaker's slippers, mauve slippers with heels, and feathers in front. She would appear at last, her face powdered white, her curled carroty hair covering her forehead and ears, the eternal jet necklace round her neck:

" Hullo, Saddika! What brings you here? "

" I was looking for work."

" I have no work for you, my poor soul."

How could she tell her after that, that she wanted the key of that room? The dressmaker was a busybody; she would be curious and ask a lot of questions. The old woman nevertheless went on walking towards the flats. The place suited her for another reason also: the cul-de-sac was used as a parking place for carts and Saddika said to herself that hers would not be noticed there. " I'll wait for her nephew, the student. He comes down early, I'll ask him for the key. Men are less suspicious."

Agitated by these thoughts, she no longer noticed the effort of pushing the cart, nor the pains in her cramped arms.

Om Hassan was going along at a good pace, when as she turned the corner of a jeweller's shop someone spoke to her. She pretended not to hear. The voice spoke again. Someone got up to follow her. She turned and threw a glance over her shoulder. An arm, a hand was stretched out from a mass of rags. Quickly she took a coin of small value from her pocket and threw it at the beggar's feet. But he continued to follow her. " It's a policeman in

disguise." She was petrified with fear. It was only
when she saw the man hesitating at the edge of the
pavement that she understood he was blind. She
rested the shafts of her cart on the ground, and
approaching the beggar stooped to pick up the
money. Then she placed it inside his palm; holding
the beggar's hand from underneath and closing his
horny fingers over the coin.

"Oh compassionate one, I do not know your
face, I have not heard your voice, but I can guess!
I can guess!"

The blind man continued to praise her in a loud
voice until long after she had disappeared.

*
* *

The dawn gilded the walls. Among the leaves of a
huge banyan-tree planted in the middle of the little
square the birds were awake.

Saddika could not avoid jolting the cart as she
pushed it along the cul-de-sac; her stomach was
torn with the idea of the suffering which the child
was enduring from it. Right at the end stood a
wooden hut with a green signboard, a sheet of zinc
broken in two with each half still hanging to a nail,
on which was inscribed the name of a lemonade.
Because of the epidemic and the ban on fizzy drinks,
the lemonade-seller had abandoned the place. Om
Hassan pushed open the door of the empty hut and
returned to fetch the child.

Slowly removing the covering, she revealed
Hassan: and seeing him, she began to tremble. The

child lay motionless, curled up like a dog. In order to stifle his own groans he had stuck both his fists over his mouth; there were huge brown rings round his eyes. Saddika's arms, her legs would no longer obey her. " Come, come . . . He has no one but you. Come! " she said to herself.

She lifted up the child and carried him inside. Then setting him on the ground she leaned his back against a red-painted box full of empty Coca-Cola bottles.

" Wait for me here; I'm going to look for a room where we'll be safe. Don't cry out, don't call me; you mustn't be heard. I'll come back."

She looked at him imploringly; the child nodded. The slightest movement cost him an immense effort.

" What a lot of patience there is in us," thought the woman, shutting the door behind her and going towards the nearest building. " What a lot of patience there is in us and in our children! "

She climbed the three steps and went in. The inside walls, blistered and covered in places with graffiti and gashes, had not been repainted since they had been built nearly forty years ago.

The woman sat down on the bench where Ali the one-eyed porter used to sit. He had been dead for several months and no one else had as yet replaced him. Ali had been a saintly man who muttered prayers endlessly, and Saddika, watching and waiting under the well of the stairs, sent him a request for help in the hope that he could hear her wherever he might be.

The dawn burst open like a bud, flooding the cul-de-sac and the entrance to the block of flats and halting on the fringe of the dark zone which surrounded her seat. Only Om Hassan's feet were bathed in its brightness. She slipped them out of their sandals and stared at them; they were yellow and shining and seemed as though they were separate from her body. Then her vigil began, long and grievous, made doubly so by the thought of the other vigil endured by the child. Anxiously watchful at the slightest sound, she hoped each time to recognise the student's footsteps.

An hour passed by in this way. Her body held upright, her hands folded in her lap, she waited patiently.

A baker bearing on his head loaves of bread knotted into a white napkin came up the steps whistling. He deposited his two bundles on the floor a few paces from Om Hassan, blew his nose noisily between his fingers, resumed his load and climbed up to the suite on the first floor. One after the other the doors opened on to the landings.

Soon afterwards the young man came down. Saddika knew him well; she had seen him grow up.

" Who's calling me? " asked the student, just as he was crossing the threshold.

" Don't you recognise me? "

He turned towards the well of the stairs.

" I can't see you. Come nearer— "

She came forward:

" I'm the washerwoman. "

" I recognise you now. Where have you been all this time? Is it because of the cholera we don't see you any more? "

" Yes, because of the cholera— "

" That's all finished now. Happily everything passes."

" Yes, everything passes— "

" Go and see my aunt; she'll give you some work."

" It isn't her, it's you I want to see."

" Me? "

" Look: I have no house any more—mine has fallen in. I need shelter, for two or three days; then I'll return to my family in the country. Can you lend me the room upstairs? "

" I'll go and see. We'll go together— "

" Listen," she interrupted him. " What's the use of discussing it? Madame Naïla needn't know anything about it; she only goes up to the roof-garden on Thursdays. On Thursday I shall be far away. I will have put the key back under the doormat."

The student looked at his watch. It was time to go. The key was kept in the hall, at the bottom of a Chinese vase; no one would notice its disappearance. The woman was right, why talk it over?

" All right. Wait here."

The old woman bent forward, and seizing the young man's hand tried to kiss it.

" No, no, don't do that," he said, sharply withdrawing it.

He disappeared behind the corner of the first

landing. She heard him climbing the steps four at a time.

*
*   *

Saddika clasped the key in her palm while the student went away.

" By the way, where is the child? " he asked her, before he left the cul-de-sac.

" I'm going to fetch him— "

" Does he still have that mischievous expression? "

" He's full of mischief. He knows more than I do."

" It's the lamb which teaches the sheep to graze," replied the young man, who loved proverbs.

He turned round again to ask:

" Do you send him to school? "

" Of course. Later on he will be somebody! "

" Yes, of course."

This time he went away.

The student did not like hurrying. As he went round the square with the banyan-tree in it, he counted the horse-drawn cabs with their sleepy drivers drawn up in a circle round the raised strip of ground. Farther on he raised his head to look back at the yellow block of flats. The young girl in a kimono was not on her balcony; nevertheless each time he came and went he saw her; the weight of her body resting on the balustrade, her gaze fixed and far way. What was she waiting for? For motionless time suddenly to get a move on? Perhaps one evening he would make a sign to her? Merely to find out what would come of it. But nothing would happen; he was certain of that in advance. Nothing ever happened there. The days sank down, one into the other. A wave of indignation would seize you like a great black rage, snap you up in one bite and then lie down again.

Certain people experienced, in fits and starts, the need for an awakening—but of what sort? The necessity of a change—but in which direction? Then the urge was dissipated in the course of a stroll, of a conversation, in the banality of meeting people, and was put off until tomorrow. Why was it so difficult to persevere? It seemed as though one was advancing into the middle of a tide of humanity, moved by vague dreams, hazy desires, projects that were never carried out. Hope lost its vigour. A soft and easy boredom stuck to your skin. The soil of that country was heavy. So heavy.

*
* *

Violently shivering, his arms and legs splayed out in every direction, the child had slid to the ground. Om Hassan's entry, however, seemed to calm him. She lowered herself to sit on her heels; ever since yesterday her body had obeyed her as though it were no longer old. The child's breathing was fast, uneven; his tongue hung out of his mouth. He was thirsty.

" I've found the room! On the roof, far away from everyone. We will be safe. There is a tap and some water! " She was panting with impatience. " All the water you want. You'll drink and get well, my soul! "

She wrapped him in a worn blanket and lifted him up. He seemed to be lighter than before.

" Now I'm opening the door. We're in the cul-de-sac; there are some people over there but they have their backs turned to us. Here are the flats." During the journey she did not stop talking to him, as though they had to do everything together. " I'm going upstairs; one, two—you don't feel too bad? " He pressed himself against her; she felt his burning breath through the stuff of her bodice. " It's not much farther."

To give herself courage, she pictured the room with its whitewashed walls and brass tap. One only had to turn it and clear water squirted out full of bubbles. " I'll wash you and you'll drink . . ." With this idea she felt herself enveloped in freshness. " Only three more floors . . ." A couple came out on to the landing she had just left, having an argument. A door banged and another opened. The old woman pressed on; but the child began to weigh heavily and she stopped to take her breath a little. Approaching the rail, she leant over and looked up: " Only two more floors . . ." It seemed as though she would never finish the ascent. The child clung to her as if he were sinking down. " Come," she said, " it'll soon be over." She began to count the steps. Her legs were as heavy as lead. " Only ten more . . ." Then out loud: " Five, four . . . two, one." On the last step she was left with just enough strength to lift with her elbow the latch which opened the door on to the roof.

Outside on the flat roof she leant her back for a long moment on the parapet.

All around her other roof-gardens stretched in disorderly confusion out of sight; a few rooms like cabins rose up among a confusion of scrap iron and old pieces of furniture. Farther away one could see islands of greenery; farther off still the crowded poorer quarter, lying in flat brown stains on the outskirts. To the east the desert mountain chain of Mokatam dominated the town, holding back the ocean of sand which was sometimes unleashed to blow over the city in reddish winds.

In the room, everything was in its place: the cistern, the primus, a cake of soap, the rod for stirring the boiling linen. The white walls reflected the light, the tap sparkled: it was the colour of gold, but more beautiful, livelier than gold, with its dangling drop of water.

" We are saved! Do you understand, little one, we are saved! "

PART II

CHAPTER 1

THE twilight softened the outlines, lulled the river and the trees, coloured the stones pink, when Okkasionne, the man with the performing monkey, appeared at the top of the steps of the Ministry of Health and began walking slowly down them. He held a ten-pound note in an ostentatious way between his thumb and forefinger; he let it flutter a moment in the breeze. Then he shook it close to his ear and delighted in its rustling.

Ten pounds! Never had he possessed such a sum all at once before. Next he examined its green paper. It was smooth, satiny, fresh from the press; he must surely be its first owner. In order to free his other hand, the busker slipped his malacca cane under his belt, then flicked the centre of the note with his fingers. It gave a dry crackle which overwhelmed him with pleasure.

" Mangua, my monkey! " said he to his wistiti with its bald, scarlet bottom, perched on his shoulder. " God be praised, we're not so foolish as we seem, you and I! "

Furthermore the official had congratulated him for his patriotic and humanitarian deed on behalf of the Minister himself. He had even added: " The newspapers will write about you and hold you up as an example. Without naming you, of course, so that you can go on with what you're doing in peace."

" Mangua, my daughter, long live the cholera!
I'm like the onion which gets into everything, but,
alas, this time I understood too late what was good
for us. It's a pity the epidemic is coming to an end.
If we had known earlier we might have been
millionaires, with a palace reaching up to the sky,
and we wouldn't have had to dance any more
except as we fancied. . . . But who knows, Mangua?
Perhaps fortune is keeping her eye fixed on us, and
we'll soon find some other cases to report."

With a bound the monkey alighted on the pavement and pulled at its chain, overcome with wild
excitement.

" Be quiet, be quiet, Mangua! Rest! I'm going to
offer you a bagful of peanuts while your master will
treat himself to a thousand puffs of the hookah,
washed down with tea that is blacker than soot."

Soon afterwards, seated in a tavern, Okkasionne
settled himself indolently in his chair. The place
was like a full box whose sides were on the point of
bursting. Through the curtain of smoke, men were
talking to each other in loud voices and from table
to table, while the waiter pushed his way through
them all with difficulty. A radio was pouring out a
stream of words interspersed with songs.

" We'll drink to our health, Mangua! " the busker
continued his monologue. " May our prosperity
last long, as long as the days of summer put end to
end. . . ."

Besotted with the food, the smell and the noise,
the monkey had curled up at its master's feet

beside a pile of empty nutshells and hid its muzzle in the long blue robe.

*

* *

Towards midnight Okkasionne got up and went out.

With a carefree step, followed by the animal, which he had retied to his belt by a supple chain with large rings, he walked towards the garden of the grottoes, beside whose railings he intended to sleep that night.

In order to reach it he cut across the residential district. The gardens slept softly under a domed sky dotted with stars. Passing between two tall white blocks of flats with green shutters, near where he sometimes came to beg, the busker paused and gazed up at them for a long time. During this halt, the wistiti, having sniffed at its surroundings, and recognised them, began dutifully executing a series of knowing capers.

" Mangua, delight of my eyes, my star! Jump! " said Okkasionne, patting himself on the thighs. " You have a sound in your throat, you must sing it. . . . Jump as high as the moon if you want to! But this evening, remember, it's only for your own pleasure. Tonight we ask for nothing. He who needs nothing is free. We are free. Do you understand me, free! No one in this town is freer than us! "

But after a few seconds, as though his own blood were on fire, the busker rehearsed his usual piece. Pivoting on his bent legs, beating on the drum hung from his waist, twirling his cane in the other hand, he beamed with such a big smile that his face seemed split in half. His screwed-up eyes disappeared under his projecting forehead and thick eyebrows.

Mangua turned in rapid circles, jigged up and down, raised her faded cap, shook her neck to tinkle the three bells fixed to her leather collar, showed her yellow teeth.

" Mangua, my beauty . . ." hummed the busker softly, drawing the monkey round after him. " Look at your master! You see before you a wealthy and patriotic man. Did you think it would be so easy to be an esteemed citizen? I please the great ones of this world, Mangua. In a short time, and if God lends the cholera a little more life, our fortune will be made! "

The moon shone brilliantly down from a sky which grew darker and darker.

A few late diners leant over a balcony. Some piastres, accompanied by bursts of talking and laughter, fell into the street.

In the building on the left, a bay-window was lit up. A woman clad in a dressing-gown appeared framed in the window and greeted the group of diners opposite with a friendly gesture. Then she disappeared only to return at the end of a few seconds, and let her hand hang over the window-ledge to release a trickle of innumerable small coins.

Another, and then another window opened. Very soon the two buildings were pierced with luminous holes. From one floor to the other, from one block

of flats to the other, the occupants exchanged
joking remarks; their voices, their applause criss-
crossed between them. Nobody thought of driving
the intruder away.

" What gaiety this evening, what good humour!
And they all know each other. . . . It's true," continued the busker, " that their world is not as crowded
as ours is. Calamities and crowds! Is there an over-
flow which brims over on to us without ceasing? If
the sky and the stars were shaken up, children and
misfortunes would still rain down on our
shoulders! " At any other time a porter or a servant
would have chased the busker away as soon as he
began beating his drum. " Hey, you down there
with your monkey, be off with you! " Whereas this
evening . . . " Listen, Mangua, they are applauding
me! I am king. Their king. The king of the
buffoons! No day is like the one before," he proclaimed at last. " Man is like a tree, my beauty,
sometimes clothed, sometimes unclothed! " He
lifted his arms majestically as though he were all at
once growing branches and myriads of leaves all
over his body. " And do you know," this time he
spoke confidentially, "I could dry up the laughter on
their lips if I cried out the truth: 'The cholera is still
within your walls!' That's what I could call out.
I've seen a case of cholera myself and not very far
from here either. Death is still within your walls. It
is still on our faces. I see it everywhere! "

He burst into peals of laughter while continuing
his dumb show. His arms were held out now like
wings. Then the man spun round on his heel, the

hem of his robe coiling round his ankles, and finished with a magnificent pirouette.

" That's enough for now," he said, addressing his partner.

But the people up above did not want to get rid of him:

" Encore! Encore! Beat your drum. Dance! "

He behaved as though he did not hear them. " The disease of the dirty hands," he muttered to himself. " That's what they call the cholera. . . . They don't fear anything themselves; they have clean hands." He stooped down, picked up a quantity of small coins from under the street-lamps and looked at them glistening on his grey palm. He then caught the monkey and forced it to open its fist already full of piastres. " You've got hands just like a cholera case yourself!" he roared with laughter. Then ceremoniously after having pocketed the money, he smacked a noisy kiss into the little wrinkled hand, while Mangua gave piercing cries.

On the first-floor balcony, couples were entwined to the sound of music coming from inside the flat, which could scarcely be heard from the street. A fat, bald-headed man struggled feebly while a blonde with a shrill voice emptied the recesses of his pocket in order to tip the contents over the balustrade. Then she seemed to stumble, and fell on top of her victim.

" They're drunk," the busker said to himself, " they too want to forget. . . . But what, what do they lack? " With his hands on his hips, he contemplated the flats once more; and then gazed all along the pavement at the row of big-bellied cars with large chromium-plated teeth. " What do they lack? Eh, Mangua, my mouse," said he, addressing the monkey. " D'you want me to tell you? They have too much of everything; they possess so much that they themselves are possessed. . . . They're smothered in it! But we're not going to do the same. We pick up what we find on the ground and go on our way. . . . Enough's enough! Even if after that they threw us gold, we would go away."

Never before had Okkasionne collected so much.

" What was I saying to you, Mangua? This evening we're fate's darlings, fortune's favourites. We only have to show ourselves to be drowned in beautiful silver money! At other times, eh, my beauty, I dance until I burst under a sun which pierces through my skull, and you jump until you don't know which is the air and which is the ground. I can beat my drum until my fingers are broken; you spin round fast enough to unscrew your head, and not one of that future carrion throws me a farthing. . . . There are evenings, Mangua, there are evenings like this one—when we had nothing but a stick of celery to divide between us and empty bellies—there are evenings when our luck is such a kind old man one can sit on his knees and examine his beard. And there are evenings when one can signal for a piece of the sky to fall down before he will allow one anywhere near him. . . . But don't be afraid, Mangua, honey, the sky can stay where it is. For my part I prefer to stay here with you. In short, this town suits me better than any paradise! "

Some more piastres had rolled under the cars. The monkey slipped in and out under the wheels to get them. He came out covered with black grease.

"We'll be going," said Okkasionne, when nothing more was left on the ground, and kneeling on one knee he made a sign to Mangua to jump on to his shoulder.

Straightening up, holding his head high, he walked away with measured steps as though he were bringing up the rear of a procession. Behind them their shadows lengthened out like an immense black train.

Just as they were branching off in the direction of the gardens, the busker heard a clinking sound. One, two, three, five pieces had struck the soil. He hesitated, slackened his pace. Should he retrace his steps?

"We're free, Mangua," said he at last, his face lifted towards his monkey. "We've said: 'We are going', and we will go."

Someone called to him:

"Why, you fool, you're leaving money all over the place behind you!"

Three more coins tinkled down.

This time Okkasionne shrugged his shoulders, and without even troubling to reply continued on his way.

CHAPTER 2

THE same twilight was falling on Om Hassan, who had not left the laundry-room all day. The oil lamp, standing on the floor just under the brass tap gave a feeble light and crowded the room with shadows.

The night seemed to turn to stone around the sleeping child. A night which was more unbearable than the one before. The woman missed the effort of pushing the cart; she was alone, cruelly alone, between these walls, whitewashed like a cemetery's.

She got up and remained standing for a long time with folded arms. Then for something to do, she started pushing the pump of the lamp in and out. A hot light flooded the walls and ceiling with glowing suns. She looked round her as though she had risen up out of a well.

But, noticing that the light worried the child—he moaned, his face creased, his eyelids blinked, he turned from side to side—the old woman at once tried to soften the rays by turning the handle a screw, and plunging the room little by little into semi-darkness again.

For several hours she had not dared make Hassan drink. He could no longer hold down a single mouthful; at the slightest touch of a wet cloth his whole body shivered. Nevertheless he was thirsty, and his teeth were covered with a gummy coating.

The old woman returned to sit beside him, after throwing an angry glance at the tap, which shone brighter now than during the day and seemed to snap its fingers at them.

" He looks like Saïd," she thought, fixing her gaze on the child's face. The same forehead grooved with little furrows, and the deep lines on either side of his mouth. His skin seemed too large for him everywhere; the woman did what she could to make the net of wrinkles disappear, by smoothing it with the tips of her fingers. " He looks like a dry, blue prune." Only his eyes came to life in flashes, letting through a keen and tragic glance. After a moment he spoke:

" I'm going to die."

" Don't say that."

" To die . . ." he went on.

" It isn't true."

" My teacher is dead and I'm going to die," he went on in a broken voice.

" Your teacher had no one to look after him. . . . You have me."

" I'm going to die like my teacher."

She did not believe he could hear her any more, but she still insisted:

" Neither men nor death shall take you away from me."

" I'm going to die, it's like that . . ." Hassan persisted.

" It's not like that." She must stop him being so resigned. She bent low enough to brush his moist cheeks, and received the child's fetid breath full in her nostrils. "You're my life," she whispered to him without drawing back. "Do you hear? You're my life."

"There's a sound like bells in my ears, like hundreds of wasps in my ears. . . . I know I'm going to die."

"No, no," cried the woman.

Raising her arms she crossed them violently several times before her. It was as though she were signalling to someone at a distance on the other side of a river; as though they were separated by a great stretch of water, which prevented her voice from carrying.

"No, no," said she, more softly.

The child grew silent, and seemed to sink down into heavy sleep. Bent over him, the old woman examined his features. How could that face, which had been as round and full as a fresh fruit, have so quickly become this shrivelled-up thing?

"Not him, not him . . . it's not fair." It had taken her and Saïd a whole lifetime for their flesh to become as ugly as that. All at once she pictured her bosom when she was a young girl, her breasts hard as though held up from within, her belly her hips like the earthenware of the jars smooth from the potter's hands. Then she saw herself as she had become, with her breasts like waterskins on the point of cracking the fragile skin, her huge, blackish nipples, her thighs criss-crossed with broken veins, her clotted calves. "Old age is a field that has been many times ploughed, and God knows, that's as it should be . . . but a child!" Slowly she lifted

Hassan's tunic, uncovering his stomach; it was flattened in the shape of a boat with flabby skin hanging round it: "the stomach of a corpse," she thought, covering it again immediately.

The tap gurgled insistently. Om Hassan went up to it and wetted a cloth; then once again she strove to make the child drink. But at the mere sight of the rag he vomited again. What he threw up was full of mucus. A smell of old pickling brine invaded the room, and the woman saw again the reed hut, her nephews manipulating the dead woman, the bunch of onions hanging from the ceiling, the half-crazy little girl, gnawing her nails . . .

"It's nothing, little one, it's nothing . . ." she muttered, as though her lips no longer belonged to her.

*

*   *

Piercing the attic window, the moon's rays caused the tap to glow like a flame. Saddika advanced a few steps and spat a jet of saliva on to the brilliant metal.

The child was motionless. Had he given up living? And she, had she given up for him? Despair was all around her, watching her, cowering in every corner of the room. It had a hairy body, spider's feet; it would suddenly pounce on her and entangle her in its net.

Suddenly the woman stood up; even her clothes were too heavy for her, she made a movement of her shoulders as though to throw them off. Now she was turning the key, she was opening the door, she was going out on to the roof.

A gentle puff of wind swelled her dress, made it less heavy. A breeze slid into her long sleeves, caressed her arms, slipped under the veil along her temples, penetrated under her hair.

All round it was night. It was still night. How she and the child were dedicated to the night. " Oh thou who dissipateth sadness . . ." To whom was she speaking?

Was there anyone to hear her? Only to be able to go out at night, when there were nothing but stones to talk to, when the sky looked like a slab of wood fastened together with yellow nails. The old woman leant with her elbows on the parapet. " A great town and no one to listen to me! " If only someone could come up. No matter who, so as to see a face. . . . Saïd or the student or even Zakieh the neighbour, or Madame Naïla who would be asleep downstairs, with her red hair, and her long jet necklace round her neck. " If I cry out loud enough . . . if I call to all the mothers in this town, they'll come . . . Look at me, I'm going mad! I shall end up in the asylum."

She left the roof-garden and went back into the room.

*

*　*

Squatting down, her back to the wall, she laid her two hands flat on the child's stomach. An ageless peace settled on her, ran through her veins.

" On the sixth day Hassan will be restored to life." The boy lying there is only an image, an image of the child of tomorrow. Today is nothing because tomorrow is coming. Four days from now the child will have stopped vomiting, he will ask for something to drink, he will drink. His pulse will beat strongly, his veins will fill with blood, his skin will get warm again. He will recover his child's smell."

The old woman began softly singing, modulating her voice in the way Hassan loved:

" How many birds are there in the sky?
One for the baby
One for marriage
One for the crops
One for the good child.

How many trees are there on the earth?
One for healing
One for old age
One for every boy's life
One for the journey."

Wrapped up to his chin in a piece of chequered material, the child was breathing noisily. The old woman, having grown used to this hurried breathing since the night before, believed she could leave him without too much risk, and go and wait for the student in the cul-de-sac. She feared a visit from him more than anything else. What could she do, if he came up, to hide the child from him in this bare room?

Midday struck and all was quiet on the roof-garden. It contained only seven laundry-rooms, separated one from the other and only used at the end of the week.

But just as the woman turned the handle of the door, she heard a noise. She listened. The foot-steps went away and then came back again. Some-one was walking backwards and forwards outside her room. No doubt they were trying to spy on her? She took the great key out of the lock and looked through the keyhole. A man, fat and short in the legs, a long cigarette clutched between thumb and forefinger, was smoking it with little jerky move-ments. She recognised this tic and also the face pitted by smallpox.

The old woman thought the grocer looked even uglier than a few months ago. He flaunted a tussore jacket with glossy lapels. Round his ridiculously short legs hung a pair of striped pyjama trousers. He wore impeccably polished reddish buttoned boots. From time to time he pulled a watch out of his waistcoat pocket, gazed at it, replaced it and went on walking up and down. At last he shot out a curse and departed in the direction of the stairs. But as he reached the door of the roof-garden it opened from the inside.

Then everything happened very quickly, almost on top of Saddika's room. She saw a skirt the colour of a scarlet poppy, a pair of young, sturdy legs, one of them marked with a wart on the calf, rubbing themselves against the limp material of the pyjamas. The polished boots were wedged against sandals with worn straps, disclosing slender ankles. A note fluttered to the ground; with a brisk movement the girl pinned it under her heel. Her shrill laugh and the man's choppy breathing penetrated the walls.

Om Hassan turned round, her hands pressed over her ears and leant her back against the door, searching for the child with her eyes.

His thin face surrounded with rags was serious. So white, so frail, so serious. . . .

Outside the door they were still laughing.

*
*   *

The couple had vanished. There was nothing left of their presence on the roof-garden but footprints and cigarette stubs. Saddika ground one of them under her heel.

She met no one on the stairs and went out of the building. The sun beat down on the cul-de-sac, but the children were amusing themselves running about with their satchels still on their backs, without feeling any discomfort. Artim, the eldest son of the Armenian tailor, recognised the old woman standing on the steps, and came up to her to ask where Hassan was and if he would like to join them. Not knowing what to answer, she rummaged in the bottom of her deep pocket and found some preserved dates which she offered him. He took them and ran away.

While she was going towards the place where the carts were parked, Om Hassan was struck full in the skirt by a tennis ball of whitish, shaved felt.

" Throw it," cried a child's voice.

" Yes, throw it—hard! "

Holding it in the hollow of her hand, the woman could not help thinking of Hassan's fingers, too weak to close over anything.

" Go on, go on—" clamoured the voices.

She raised her voice and looked up towards the roof-garden. " If I throw the ball with all my strength, perhaps it will reach the attic window, perhaps Hassan will see it . . . " Then she said to herself that the sight of this ball would remind the child of happy memories. She imagined his smile.

" Go on, Om Hassan! "

The old woman concentrated. Putting her arm behind her, she leaned backwards sharply and in one movement sent the ball vertically upwards.

It stopped in mid-course; fell back like a stone between Artim's outstretched hands.

*

*   *

She found other carts standing beside her own; one of these had a little donkey harnessed to it, wearing a blue horse-collar adorned with red pompons. Round its big eyes, bordered with moist black rings, flies had glued themselves. The animal's patience appeared to have no limit, but sometimes, overcome with sudden fury, it shook its head and struck the ground with its hoofs, before falling back into its tenacious apathy. Om Hassan lingered beside the animal, caressing it between its ears, scratching its neck, chasing away the flies.

Then she knocked the rails and wheels of her cart to test its solidity; no doubt she would soon have to use it again. After a moment she noticed a little girl sucking a melon rind, sitting under the body of her vehicle. Hearing a noise, the child stretched out her hand to beg for alms with a mechanical gesture. Her fingers were sticky, with yellow pips stuck to the joints. As nothing fell into her palm, she withdrew it and quietly went on sucking the fruit.

" There's nothing more to eat on it," said the woman.

The little girl burst out laughing. She wore a dirty grey dress which came down to her ankles.

" Are you still hungry? "

" I'm always hungry."

She came out of the shade on all fours. The old woman noticed her healthy, shining teeth, her fleshy lips, her smooth skin.

" Who looks after you? "

" No one. There are fourteen of us at home."

" Come," said Saddika, after she had made sure the student was not yet there. " I've got a little time to spare."

Taking the little girl by the hand, she led her as far as the grocery. The grocer was dozing behind his counter, a huddled heap of fat, his tussore jacket hung on a nail. His assistant was slackly sweeping the floor, pushing the refuse into the street. At the back of the shop, a huge pan of beans was cooking over a tiny flame.

" Give us some beans in a loaf of bread and some raw onions."

" So you're back in the quarter," said the grocer, scarcely raising his eyelids, " I will tell my wife so that she can give you her washing."

Om Hassan did not take her eyes from the cul-de-sac.

" Take this," she said to the little girl, when the young assistant had served her.

" And you, aren't you going to eat? "

She paid.

" I don't want anything," she said.

The child took the loaf, shifted it several times from one hand to the other, smelled it; then applied it to her cheek to feel its exquisite warmth. Om Hassan suddenly had the impression that the little girl was rotting away before her eyes. Her cheeks were being eaten from within, her face was absorbed into itself, her skin softened round the neck, her teeth turned yellow. . . .

She gave a cry and brusquely left the shop.

The school-children were forming a ring in the centre of the cul-de-sac. Their faces were blue and wrinkled, their clothes floated about their skeleton bodies. They encircled the woman and began dancing around her and singing about death. Saddika turned round and round, trying to escape from them. Suddenly she broke the chain of their arms and ran towards the block of flats.

As she ran, she knocked into the young girl with the poppy-coloured skirt, who shrugged her shoulders and went on her way, the heels of her sandals tapping against the soles of her feet.

Just as she was disappearing from sight, the little girl caught Om Hassan by the hem of her skirt.

" Why are you going? "

" Go away! Don't touch me."

The little girl drew back frightened.

*

* *

" Om Hassan! Don't go away," the student called suddenly, " I was going up to see you."

The old woman turned round and gazed at him without speaking.

" What's the matter with you? Are you ill? "

" Those children won't leave me in peace. . . . I was going to wait inside, on the seat."

He threatened the school-children with his raised arm:

" If they bother you they'll have me to deal with."

" I came to tell you that you'll find the key under the doormat the day after tomorrow," she said.

" Will you be coming back later? "

" Yes, later on I'll come back."

He held out his hand, but she made as though she had not noticed it. Ever since a short while ago she had seen death everywhere. She did not want to touch anyone any more.

The student went away. Om Hassan waited a moment, sitting on the steps.

A clock was heard striking the hour.

The children disappeared in a flash. There was no one left but the woman in the deserted cul-de-sac.

CHAPTER 4

SADDIKA stood up. She had started climbing up to the sixth floor again when she heard someone calling her:

" Eh! Om Hassan, may your day be plentiful! "

The voice seemed familiar to her. Descending a step, she looked about her without seeing anyone. Then at the corner of the nearest building, she caught sight of a huge stick, painted white and decorated all the way down with garlands. This object touched the ground and rose again, twirling round in circles.

" Who's calling me? " she cried.

The rod was soon followed by a pair of scarlet Turkish slippers. The old woman descended a second step and bent forward to see better. At last the man appeared dressed in a blue silk robe covered with a wide, embroidered cloak, and carrying on his shoulder a monkey clad in dazzling colours.

" Here we are! " he announced, pausing as though making an entry on to the stage.

" Okkasionne! " exclaimed the old woman, who had known him for a long time.

" What are you doing in these parts, woman? "

" I'm looking for work. . . ."

" For work! "

The man shrugged his shoulders, and placing his wand on the ground pulled a new flute out of his sash. Then he began blowing into the instrument and parading up and down in the empty cul-de-sac. His cloak floated behind him, swelling out like a tent; while the monkey, standing up with its hand round its master's head, spread out its pink satin skirt. They were both wearing quilted yellow skull-caps.

For fear of a crowd gathering, Saddika kept making signs to him to stop his music:

" This isn't the right district for you. . . . You won't collect anything here."

He paused, draping himself entirely in his gleaming cloak with its blue ground strewn with red stars:

" Take a look old woman, and say if you don't think us beautiful."

" Very beautiful," she replied, trying to cut him short.

" I've taken my monkey to the barber; look, her coat is now clipped like a lawn. Afterwards we chose our clothes. . . . The salesmen made a great fuss of us, bowing and trying to please us as though we were shareholders."

The woman drew back, anxious to get away.

" What, aren't you going to ask me where I got so much money? "

" That's your business."

" But where are you going? Why are you in such a hurry? "

" I have something to do."

" To do? At this hour? All work must come to an end, sometime, Om Hassan! Anyone who says otherwise is a liar and goes against the laws of

God. . . . " He waited for an answer which did not come. " You're in too much of a hurry and you aren't curious enough. It isn't normal for a woman. . . . And an old woman at that."

" Let me go," she insisted.

He came nearer. When he was quite close, he bent his knees a little and looked up at her from below.

" If you don't want to come with me, I'll go with you, aunt."

" Very well," said she, " I'll stay a moment."

" Look how easily persuaded she is! Now, ask me questions."

" What questions? "

" You know very well. . . . Ask me how I got all this money."

" How did you get all this money? " she asked, without conviction.

Then, holding her by the elbow, he told his story. " The cholera," he concluded, " is a gold mine. If I'd known . . ." He then proposed they should work together. " You go round a good deal, you could tell me the names of any people who are hiding their sick. . . . If there are any left! " he sighed. " You see it's a piece of good luck which has brought us together." As she said nothing, he went on: " As for today, I've found something else. I've heard there's a big wedding in the town. If we hurry, we shall be at the doors of the church for the beginning of the ceremony. Purse strings are easily loosened on these occasions! "

" I never beg," she dryly replied.

" Who said anything about begging, woman?

I don't beg either. I put on a show and you collect the money. . . . That's all."

" I haven't the time. I'm looking for work. . . ."

" And I'm looking for your good. Come on, why are you so obstinate? For an hour; only an hour. You must look higher than yourself, otherwise you finish up like the slug, crawling on the ground."

Taking her by the hand, he dragged her along with him. She let herself be persuaded for fear of arousing his suspicions. Once in the town she would take advantage of the crowds to get away.

" Go on, I'm following you."

At once he let go of her hand and walked in front of her with a lively step.

" Om Hassan," he exclaimed, turning round from time to time, " you are the lady of ladies. My word, you're worth more than all the others we shall see walking by."

*
* *

When they were five hundred yards from the cul-de-sac, Okkasionne caught sight of a tram—which already overflowed with a tightly packed crowd of passengers—and pushed the old woman on to it:

" We're late," he panted, climbing on to the steps behind her.

Followed by the busker, Om Hassan slipped into the middle of the crowd. Two veiled women saw her and made room for her to sit down between them, while Okkasionne stood up grasping a strap, which hung from the roof. By means of his shoulders and elbows the conductor laboriously pushed his way through. He was stifling in a khaki uniform with rolled-up sleeves and half-open neck. His red cap, too large for his skull and held up by his ears, gave him a contrite air, which was accentuated by a drooping moustache with hairs as coarse and dry as straw. Stopping in front of the women, he thumbed through his tickets, with the sweat streaming down his cheeks.

" I'm paying for the one with the uncovered face," brayed the busker.

People were clustered on the steps, clinging to the roof, the doors, the iron bars, like a swarm of ants.

In a cacophony of glass panes and old iron, the vehicle jolted along towards the heart of the city. The streets became avenues, the pavements grew wider. Imposing buildings succeeded the decayed blocks of flats, and large stores the little shops. The sky appeared more spacious. The bushes grew more numerous, although they still looked like eternal convalescents. In places their bark was swollen out and split as though under the pressure of a prolonged drought.

The old woman was haunted by the child's face. Suddenly it broke up like glass into a thousand tiny pieces; there was nothing left of it but the lips. The lips were dry, grey, cracked. The woman thrust forward her mouth, as though applying it to her grandson's so that he might share its humidity and freshness.

The tram's stopping wakened her sharply from her dream.

" Here it is," cried the busker. " Well, aunt! Are you getting down?"

In respect for her age, they made way for her to get past, and while he helped her to alight the conductor directed her towards Okkasionne.

" Take her," said he, placing the monkey in her arms, " I'm lending you Mangua! "

Then he went on in front, letting the chain come unwound between them.

*

* *

Okkasionne knew the town as though he had built it. He also knew the names of the streets and the shops and even the owners of the blocks of flats. It was unusual for a face to be totally unknown to him.

Dragging the old woman after him—the end of the long chain going from the monkey's collar to his own belt—the busker slipped in and out and all over the place. He greeted Fattal, the dwarf who sold lottery tickets. Then he spoke encouraging words to the strolling flower-seller who shook her bunches of tea-roses with dripping stalks under the noses of the passers-by. A little farther on he noticed Nabil, the hairdresser's assistant, crossing the roadway, carrying three cups of coffee on a tin tray; he emptied one of them in one go, then making his last coin ring on the metal tray:

" As for the change, you can keep it and have

yourself shaved at my expense, by the boss himself! "

Leaning with his back against the bookshop, the vendor of pins and hairnets—his merchandise arranged in a sort of open box hung round his neck —called out to him:

" Hullo, Okkasionne! What have you done with your monkey? "

" I'm as free as air! " he retorted. " I employ someone on purpose to mind Mangua! Look! "

They continued on their way. Farther on were sweet lemons, oranges, mandarins and apples from the Lebanon piled up in huge wicker baskets. A little boy was making them shine by breathing on them and wiping them with a rag. The proprietor watched him doing this with his hands folded over his stomach and a complacent expression.

" Who'll buy me an apple? " exclaimed Okkasionne.

" Give him an apple," said the man, without unfolding his arms.

" No, I'll choose one! "

The busker chose from the top of the basket a velvety fruit of the most beautiful scarlet.

" There you are," he said, handing it to Saddika, " It'll put colour in your cheeks."

She took it without a word.

" Eat it. . . ."

" I wouldn't be able to. . . ." Even the smell sickened her. " Because of my teeth," she added.

" Give it back to me, then."

He held out his hands to catch it in mid-air, then

bit into the flesh with the greatest relish. The juice trickled round his chin. "Marvellous," he exclaimed, "the fruit of paradise!" But a few steps farther on, catching sight of El Koto, the hunchbacked beggar, in front of Gelin's cake-shop—his dress raised above his right thigh as usual to expose his rachitic leg—he placed the apple in his hand and made off without waiting for thanks.

Ostentatious cars with wide mudguards splashed the street with mud. Crossing among them, the busker dealt one of their bonnets several little taps with the tip of his flute:

"You don't frighten me with your dentures!"

The man at the steering-wheel—wearing tortoiseshell spectacles and with a young, red-haired woman beside him fresh from the hairdresser—let down his window and began to blast the busker with insults. He retorted with an obscenity. Then turning to Om Hassan, who was pale as death, he advised her to hurry, if she did not want to end up in the police station with him.

"Why are you in such a hurry, Okkasionne?" the porter outside the bank called to him when he saw the strange procession going past. "Where are you going?"

"We're busy," replied the busker.

They turned off to the right.

"There's the church," said Saddika, out of breath, catching sight of the huge edifice surmounted by a cross.

CHAPTER 5

THE Franciscan church with its low wall surmounted by a high black railing now came into view above the many-coloured crowd.

Nothing seemed impossible to Okkasionne, and he forced his way through the crowd up to the porch.

" The best place or nothing at all! " he whispered to his companion.

They were pressing forward shoulder to shoulder, while Mangua in wild excitement jerked about in Om Hassan's arms, took off her quilted cap and threw it in the air, screamed and lifted up her skirts.

" You take yourself for the bride," mocked the busker.

The other people made way for the strange trio. The monkey snatched a silk scarf, tackled a flowered hat. With a brisk movement Okkasionne seized his wistiti from the old woman's arms, and holding her with her head pressed under his armpit, he threatened to shut her into his bag if she didn't keep quiet immediately. Mangua then played the corpse until her master should see fit to set her free.

" Don't let me hear another sound out of you," he scolded. " When I want you to give a performance I'll tell you. At present the comedy is to be played elsewhere; you mustn't spoil my pleasure."

He kissed the monkey on top of her head and

placed her on his shoulder. The animal kept quiet, huddled up against the nape of her master's neck.

Saddika was no longer attached to him by the chain, but she nevertheless felt a prisoner, walled in by the crowd. She was afraid of the man with the monkey, afraid of them all, afraid of giving way to complete madness.

Okkasionne was at his liveliest. His face was tense, drops of sweat pearled his forehead while he drank in the spectacle with his eyes. The great organs began to sound.

"Look," he said, suddenly pushing the woman forward by the elbow.

In a cloud of white lace, the bride was advancing along the red carpet. An elderly man with a pointed nose and a self-important torso held her by the arm. He looked at the crowd of people with a furious air, and from time to time made an authoritative gesture with his jewelled hand to them to stand back.

"A first-class wedding" exclaimed the busker, bursting with laughter. "What are they playing at? Where will they end up? At a first-class burial!" He held his nose. "I can smell the decay already. Fifty years from now we will all have returned into the belly of our mother the mud. Which class does Mother Earth belong to? Eh, Om Hassan, do you know?"

Just as she was passing in front of them the bride paused. She slowly inclined her head towards the old woman, whom she had just recognised, and smiled at her. Saddika also recognised the young girl of three days ago. But Dana had already passed by, her long train soon disappeared behind her into the church.

" What a sad face . . ." the woman was thinking.

The doors remained shut for more than an hour, and once again Saddika tried to elude the man with the monkey. But as soon as she made a movement his hand came down on her shoulder. There was no doubt he was gifted with strange powers. She forced herself to empty her expression of all uneasiness, of all thought, and show the man a smooth face. Perhaps he knew everything and was waiting for some sign of impatience from her. She would not give him that sign. She would still be patient; she would find a means of escape.

The crowd streamed out towards the street. Some boys surrounded Om Hassan and the busker and applauded Mangua, who was back again in favour, and spun round in circles up and down the stick. Other children pressed round a green shop. The cigarette-seller, participating in the general euphoria, unscrewed the lid of a fat jar and dipping in the ends of his nicotine-stained fingers distributed gum-drops.

At the end of the ceremony, as soon as the doors were opened, the neighbouring streets were quickly emptied and everyone hurried out into the square again. Only Saddika and the man with the monkey stayed behind on the edge of the pavement beside the white limousine.

" This is the best place now," the busker declared, winking his eye in the direction of the chauffeur. " We mustn't miss our chance."

Five minutes later the bridal pair did in fact return and get into the car, while Tamane held the door open for them.

Dana stared out of the window, indifferent to all that was happening round her; then she saw the old woman's face framed in it, opposite hers.

"Have you seen the bridegroom?" whispered Okkasionne. "Even Mangua wouldn't want him."

Can one be understood through a pane of glass? Om Hassan could no longer take her eyes from that face. Dana gazed back at her. From one to the other across the distance, something similar found response.

"What are you waiting for?" the bridegroom asked the chauffeur.

Tamane sounded his horn, threatened and abused the crowds which encircled the car. Okkasionne pushed the old woman to one side, and tapping on the glass with his flute, displayed his monkey and held out his hand.

Half opening the door, the bridegroom leant forward and threw a few coins into his palm.

"Monkeys bring good luck," he said to his companion.

The busker's breath had clouded the glass; now Dana could only see Mangua's dancing yellow eyes.

"Do you still want to run away?" exclaimed the man with the monkey, again seizing Saddika by the arm as she crossed the avenue.

" It's getting late. . . . I'm in a hurry."

" We've only been an hour together, old woman. Come on, come with me, you won't regret it. . . ."

There'd be no end to it all. She saw herself going on through the hours, through the weeks, through the town, the country, for ever chained to the man with the monkey. Just how far would he drag her like this? What would become of the child? She hoped he would be patient and not call out; she staked everything on his patience. But her own was at an end. At times she wished the man were dead.

" You know," continued Okkasionne, as he walked along, " people are always worth looking at; a gathering of monkeys without a keeper! Where is the keeper hiding, then? "

He stood still on the pavement without troubling about the passers-by, and pointed his forefinger with its black nail at the sky and burst out laughing. Then all at once, as though he were afraid of having overstepped some mysterious boundary and set dark forces in motion, he lowered his arm, hid his hand in his pocket and hunched his back. He might have been waiting to receive a shower of blows. As nothing happened, he went on walking.

" Where are we going? " asked Om Hassan.

" To the reception."

" What for? "

" I've thought of something."

" Do you know where it is? "

" I know everything, Om Hassan." Then he went on while Mangua rubbed herself against his cheek. " I know everything that takes place in this town. The crises, the hidden adultery, the traffic in marriages. I even know the first names of all the living and the dead. . . . I have four eyes and four ears, haven't I, Mangua, my soul? But only one tongue, which I use to good purpose."

" Why are we going there? "

" You've no imagination, woman."

Saddika could not imagine anything any more, not even the child's sufferings.

" Can't you put yourself in my hands for a few hours? Follow me and you'll see."

" Why isn't the child with you? " asked Okkasionne suddenly.

She hastened to reply:

" The old man is getting older and older; one can't leave him alone any more. The child's with him."

After covering quite a long distance, they came to a red-brick villa. A glistening white flight of steps was surmounted by a balcony supported by caryatids. Several cars which they had already seen at the church were drawn up in the street. Okkasionne went to the side entrance which led to the kitchens. He bent down and tapped on a basement window. The two halves opened to reveal a black face as round as a billiard ball.

" You come at the right moment! " said Soumba the kitchen boy, showing all his teeth in a big grin.

" I know, I know— " interrupted Okkasionne.

" You know everything," went on the kitchen boy. He had a boundless admiration for the man with the monkey, which only equalled the contempt

in which he held the cook. A man who was satisfied
with giving orders, seasoning the food with the tips
of his fingers and getting fat, while he, Soumba,
washed, swept, staggered under the weight of
baskets of provisions, scoured the pots, drew the
chickens, prepared the vegetables.

" Have you anything for us? " asked the busker
with a sweeping gesture. " There are three of us."

" When there's something for one, there's something for two, and two soon adds up to three. . . ."

Soumba took off his starched cap, and removing
the animal's bonnet he quickly changed them over
and joyfully clapped his hands.

" Very good," approved Okkasionne. " You
can be funny when you want to. I must engage you
to do a turn."

" Wait, I'll come back at once," said the kitchen
boy, eager to please him. " I'll bring you everything
I can."

" God will repay you," said the man with the
monkey.

" It's an honour to serve you."

He returned after a moment with a casserole full to
the brim with slices of meat, mixed with fish; rice,
vegetables and some fruit. Okkasionne took a tin
plate out of his bag and gave it to the old woman:

" This is to put your share on," he said. " The
child will be pleased when you go home this evening."

Mangua thrust her hand into the casserole, took
out the thigh of a chicken and rubbed it against her
teeth.

" If you begin again, Mangua, I'll hand you over to the cook," he scolded, giving her a slap. " He'll put sauce over you and serve you on a silver dish."

As he spoke, he imitated the cook, blew out his cheeks, pulled at an absent moustache, threw out his chest and seized his stomach between his two hands as though he were holding up an enormous weight.

" That's exactly like him! " roared the kitchen boy, hilariously jumping up and down.

" Come and join me this evening in the café," Okkasionne let slip in his ear. " I'll wait for you and we'll have a smoke together."

" Yes, we'll have a smoke together," repeated the kitchen boy.

Saddika, who had said nothing all the time, searched in the bottom of her pocket; there were a few dates left which she gave to the boy.

" They are from your district," she told him.

*
* *

The old woman and the man with the monkey walked along a path beside the river in the shade of thick eucalyptus trees.

Om Hassan asked herself whether Okkasionne did not know her secret, and were pushing her to the end of her endurance so that she would reveal the hiding-place of the child. If she had to, she would push the man over the top of the embankment, and then run away.

" Well, Om Hassan, you'll be able to say you

haven't wasted your day," he declared, indicating the tin plate piled with food.

" I want to ask you to do me a service," she said, struck with a sudden idea.

She put down her plate by the edge of the path, pulled out of her pocket a large handkerchief full of her savings, and spread it on the ground.

" If you help me, half of it is yours."

" It's as good as done," he returned. " Tell me what you want."

" I want to go away to the village for a few days." She searched for words. " I've got my reasons. . . ."

" Your reasons are your own," replied the busker, his eyes fixed on the handkerchief.

" Then, look, I must find a sailing-boat going towards the sea which will put me off on the way. I believe you are on good terms with the boatmen. Can you arrange this for me? "

" It's as good as done. When do you want to go? "

" Tomorrow night."

Tomorrow she had to give up the room, and the child would be nowhere safer than on the water.

" Tomorrow Abou Nawass ships his bales of cotton. I'll talk to him. He'll take you with him. Be at the corner of the green island towards midnight. You know, at the bottom of the great stone steps, at the place where the sailing-ships are moored."

With these words, he saluted her, pirouetted, and departed in the opposite direction from which they had come.

" Until then, aunt, may your day be unclouded as milk!"

" Are you sure it can be arranged?" she cried after him.

He spat on his hand:

" More than sure! By my soul, it'll be just as I've said. You needn't pay me until you have embarked. . . . Until tomorrow, Om Hassan!"

" Until tomorrow," she said, picking up the plate.

The sun slipped down, bringing relief to the sky, so that it seemed to breathe more easily and expand. Under the foliage, the less mobile shadows spread out in the shape of little lakes. The old woman turned round several times to make sure the man with the monkey was not following her. The distance made him smaller and smaller, until gradually he lost all reality.

With the monkey seated on top of his head, Okkasionne now advanced with his arms extended, imitating a funambulist walking along a tight-rope.

" Be careful you don't fall," shouted a child who was paddling in the river and had just seen the busker balancing on top of the embankment, right above him.

" Fall? Me! Don't be afraid, the earth is holding on to my feet for fear I shall take off. . . . It's an old w—— who clings to me too much."

*

* *

At the cross-roads, the woman wanted to get rid of the plate of food because its smell had become unbearable. Catching sight of a group of ragged children pressed against the front of a narrow shop, she approached them.

On the other side of the pane of glass, a man with a short beard and a head like a goat was letting fall a long thread of white syrup from a wooden basting-spoon into a basin full of jumping, steaming golden bubbles.

Tapping the most tattered of the urchins on the shoulder, Om Hassan put the plate into his hands and sped off.

CHAPTER 6

OM HASSAN feverishly ransacked the bottom of her pocket to find the key of the room. Her fingers trembled; she had to pause for a few seconds before turning the key in the lock. At last the door was opened.

Hassan had thrown off his coverings. His mottled legs were spread out in extraordinary rigidity. She called from the threshold, but he made not the slightest movement. Bending over the child, she was frightened by his drawn-back eyelids, by the suffocated appearance of his lips, by his unbelievable emaciation. With a beating heart, she knelt down to breathe into his mouth. He was still breathing. Not daring to touch him for fear that such a fragile body would fall into dust, she continued to gaze at him for a long time.

Everything seemed to encourage her to give up the struggle, to let herself crumble down on her back, like a pile of sand or dead leaves; to lie down beside Hassan. Then let death take them both! Both together, like two boats.

A hand rose up, touched her dress, trying to grasp the material. Through opaque mists, the child had suddenly felt her presence. That one gesture, although it was so frail, fired the woman with renewed life.

Sitting down, with infinite care she drew Hassan to her. The steadiness of a calm hand, of regular breathing, of a soft voice and a warm bosom, remained the only help she could still give.

Her bust arched over him as she took the child on her knees; he seemed to be composed of thin and brittle willow wands. The woman cradled him in her arms. She became a field of grass, a bed of clay. Her arms flowed like rivers round the rigid nape of his neck. Her dress between her separated thighs became a rounded valley, bearing the tragic weight of the wasted bones, the stiff legs. Her head drooped over him like a huge, fragrant flower, her bust was a tree covered with leaves.

" My king, my soul, my child who will soon be on his feet again . . ."

Hassan's eyelids again began to look like those of any other sleeping child.

" Sleep, little one, you must sleep to get across this muddy road. . . . Tonight I will watch over you; later on you will watch over me in your turn. That's the way the world goes for those who love each other. . . . Don't talk, don't move; I will talk and move for you. But listen, I tell you that you will get well. . . . The sixth day is nearly here, the sixth day approaches. A day, then another day, and it will all be over. . . . I see you (as if it were now): you are running very far in front of me along a road, and the farther away you get the larger you grow. Do you know that my legs are too worn out to follow you and there is lead and straw inside my knees? But my legs will still carry me until you are well. They'll carry me and you also as far as the water, and we'll embark tomorrow night. . . . The water heals, the water is holy. Very soon you'll wake up laughing and with a real little man's body, beside the sea. . . ."

A breath of keen and salty air invaded the room. That night the woman slept for the first time.

*
* *

The interminable day had come to an end, night was falling.

Steps, and more steps, to go down. Did life consist of nothing more than going down and climbing up again? Farther on was the sailing-boat and the sea, images which she must keep in mind.

No one was on the landings, a yellow light filtered under certain doors; not under Madame Naïla's. Om Hassan stooped and slipped the key under the mat.

Hassan was scarcely a body; she might have had nothing in her arms and it would have been the same. Nevertheless he was alive! Like the sparrows with their practically non-existent bodies. The entrance of the building, three more steps. The moon was pared round the edges, its light was cold.

Her footsteps crunched on the stones of the cul-de-sac. There was no one leaning out over the street. . . .

Yes, there was. Leaning on his elbows at his window, the student dreamed of a different world. Girls would descend from their balconies to come and meet him, people would be neither too rich nor too poor. He dreamt of journeys under unknown trees, of books which he would not write, of canvases he would never paint, of encounters . . . A woman was walking in the cul-de-sac; it was Om Hassan. What was she holding, like that? If he were to go down and give her that money he kept at the bottom of a drawer for his new suit? ' One is never generous enough.' But what an effort to go down, to call, to run. . . . And then the old woman had just that moment became merged in the night; he would never find her!

Om Hassan's heart cracked like the bark of an old tree and she looked from right to left as she advanced. She wished she could throw a veil over the moon which so cruelly laid bare the landscape; or that a wind laden with sand would arise. It would transform the town into a phantom city, it would smear people's faces with its dark grey dust so that they became unrecognisable, and each one would only seek shelter. But who could do anything to the moon? And neither the wind nor the sand listened to human beings. Saddika put one foot in front of the other, little by little her footsteps drew her away from the cul-de-sac as far as the little clearing.

Round the banyan-tree—devoured by its roots half-way up its trunk—was the parking place for horse-drawn cabs. There were two still there, with their sleeping drivers. Om Hassan was swallowed up in the huge black leather hood of the second one, completely lowered in front as in broad daylight. Inside it was like a tent.

The cab-driver snored with his forearm resting on a half ripped-open sack of lucerne. The tail of his khaki jacket overlapped the iron bar which served as a back-rest for the little seat; the woman pulled it to wake him and in a peremptory voice, imitating the tone of his clients:

" Come along, wake up, I'm in a hurry."

With a flick of his finger the man pushed up the white turban which had slipped down over his eyebrows; but he was still heavy with sleep.

" Wake up," she repeated.

" Where do you want to go? " he asked in a surly tone.

" To the green island, where the sailing-ships are moored. Do you know it? "

Without giving himself the trouble to answer, he lazily shook his whip and the horse set off.

*
*   *

The centre of the town was steeped in a festival of neon lighting and shop signs. But the black hood came down so low that the woman saw nothing—neither the opera with its luminous globes, nor the equestrian statue, nor the gardens shut for the night. By keeping still she tried to deaden the jolts of the carriage, to create a zone of calm round the child.

" Have you got enough money to pay me? " asked the cab-driver in a placid voice. But before the woman had time to answer him, he began scolding his horse, which was inclined to go at its own too rapid pace and shake up the vehicle in a manner at variance with the velvet softness of the night.

" Yes, I can pay."

Not taking any notice of his master's wishes, the horse—as though he had just discovered he had hoofs—trotted on at the same precipitate rhythm, making his shoes ring. Tired of the struggle, the driver let him go at his own pace, wagging his head and driving the animal on with a movement of his fist. On the outskirts of the town two pedestrians stopped to see the cab go rocking by along the road, swinging over the macadam, and imagined there were lovers hidden inside: " You old pimp," they shouted at the driver, " it's a shame at your age to turn your cab into a brothel! "

The child whimpered faintly, but the noise of the trotting muffled his cries. The town diminished, flattened out, receded in the distance like a large glow-worm. The road leading down to the river was badly lit and the horse was forced to slacken its pace.

The child moaned louder, and for fear of the man overhearing him, the woman began to talk. She talked out loud about all sorts of things, mixing questions and answers: the cost of living, the tourist season, the cab-driver's children; anything would do. Afraid he would think it strange of her not to mention the end of the epidemic, she even added a few sentences about the cholera.

" Enough! Enough! You are making me drunk with words," interrupted the driver. " Don't you understand you have dragged me out of a sweet sleep and I haven't completely woken up yet?"

The old woman was silent; she hoped that his sleepiness would cling to him until she had disappeared with the child. Then bending down to touch Hassan's ear, she whispered to him:

"I can smell the sails and the water!"

One of the wheels lodged against a stone, the horse stepped backward, pulled sharply and went on again. All along the stony path, the battered carriage proceeded at a funeral pace.

"Whoa!" shouted the cab-driver, pulling on the reins and drawing up on a flat strip of ground below the embankment. "Is this the place?"

"This is it."

She paid with the money which she had got ready beforehand and handed it to him from the interior of the cab. As she stepped down on to the ground, the driver struck a match to count the money.

"God keep you, O woman! Your generosity has woken me up. What's your name?"

"Om Hassan," she cried, without turning back.

"Om Hassan?"

"Yes."

"Listen carefully, Om Hassan. On the day you disembark I'll take you into the town at my own expense. Let me know when you return and I'll come. You'll find me here. It's a promise."

She began to descend the great steps. The man called her back:

" What are you carrying? Do you want me to come and help you? "

" No, no," she said, rooted to the spot.

Then the whip cracked, she heard the creaking of the wheels; the cab turned in a half circle and went off towards the city.

PART III

CHAPTER 1

A WARM breeze swelled Saddika's clothes as she descended the forty steps which lay pallid under the moon. The group of barges, fastened to the bank by their chains, floated lower down on the water. Their sails were coiled round pliant masts in the form of a bow which were extended by a longer yard. The boatmen were asleep at the bottom of their vessels. Two or three anchors lay about on the edge of the bank.

One man, still awake, stood alone barefooted on the bank and sang as he gazed at the river:

> " Over the earth and over the water
> My song will be lost
> Where the darkness is so high
> My song will be blotted out."

The footsteps came nearer. With each step she took, the woman felt lighter. The man, who was listening in spite of his singing, turned round:

" Om Hassan? "

" I'm Om Hassan."

" I'm Abou Nawass."

He was of middle height with broad shoulders and a narrow body. His blue tunic, with the ends lifted up and tucked into a belt of rope, revealed ample dark brown trousers gathered in round the ankles. A white cotton head-dress pulled down on to his ears almost entirely obscured his features.

" Welcome."

Then calling his mate who was hidden behind the cargo, he announced that as their passenger had arrived they could begin unfurling the sails. The young man sat with his feet hanging over the water, chewing maize in the bows of the felucca, and amusing himself by spitting the grains in the air and catching them again in his mouth. He grumbled that the woman had come an hour too soon, but got up all the same to do what he was told.

" I thought you would be alone," said the boatman.

" It's my grandson. He sleeps all the time; he won't bother you."

Hassan's face was hidden under a square of mosquito-netting; in the thick darkness of the night one could hardly guess the shape of his body. Saddika had purposely arrived before her appointment with the man with the monkey, thinking that she would then have time to hide the child at the bottom of the felucca.

Supporting her by the elbow, Abou Nawass helped the woman to embark. By the glow of an oil lamp placed near the helm, she could now see his face. Sun and age had marked his features without coarsening or hardening them. The man appeared to be silent, without malice, like a stranger to these shores; as though he had spent his life at sea.

" Dessouki, find a place for the child."

The young Nubian was busy round the mast.

Picking up the corn-cob which he had left on the deck, he bit into it before hailing the woman:

" This way, this way."

The old woman followed him. The bows of the boat were lined with bales of cotton; placed one on top of the other, they sometimes reached a height of ten sacks. While Om Hassan watched him with the child in her arms, Dessouki deftly shifted the bales. His rolled-up sleeves exposed his glistening black arms; with the corn-cob between his teeth, he bounded about as supple as a cat, with naked legs, picking up a bale and placing it lower down on the boards, and repeating this several times until he had formed a trench.

" Look what a place! A house, a real house for your child. He'll sleep soundly inside there."

As he went away, the young Nubian sighed and hesitated a moment before he threw his stripped cob into the water. A few seconds later he was back again disentangling the sails.

After she had removed the thin cloth, Om Hassan applied her lips to Hassan's cheek. The skin stuck to the bones; the flesh had lost its softness, the blood its warmth. Kneeling on the platform of bales, she took all the time she needed to lower his body into the bottom of the nook without shaking it. Thin and motionless, shut in between these partitions—the jute sacks were the colour of granite in the moonlight—the child made one think of some king of old, sleeping between walls of stone, awaiting the great return journey.

" Everything is going as we planned, my son," she whispered.

" Are we leaving? "

It was his voice! The child had spoken. Was it possible? A voice which had been silent for two days, a scarcely murmured breath. Although it had faded away, the woman continued to hear that voice vibrating for a long time in her head.

Overcome with gratitude towards Hassan, God, the river and the whole world, she bowed down and kissed the side of the boat.

" Yes," she replied aloud. " You will soon be well."

She leant over the hollow, expecting another answer; but this time nothing reached her. Then, lying down full length, she stretched her arm down to the bottom of the trench and put out her fingers to caress the damp forehead, the projecting cheek-bones, lingering round the mouth and chin. His face was cold. So cold that Om Hassan felt her hand freezing. A shiver rose up to her armpit and her whole body began to tremble.

*
* *

" If Okkasionne is not here soon, we'll go," said Abou Nawass, after two hours had passed.

The woman got up and called towards the stern that she owed the busker a sum of money.

" If you haven't paid him he will be here dead or alive," asserted Dessouki. " But if by chance he doesn't come, all the better for your money! "

" A debt's a debt," she rejoined.

Then bending over Hassan, she murmured to him that she was going away for a few seconds:

" Don't be afraid, I won't be long. If you can still count, count up to ten, seven times running. After that I'll be with you again."

The man with the monkey could not keep them waiting much longer; Om Hassan thought it would be better to stand near the side of the boat and hand him the money so that he would not have to come on board to fetch it.

The sail floated in the breeze, ready for departure. Nothing was to be heard except the lapping of the water against the sides of the boats, and sometimes a passing flock of birds.

" We must be going," said the boatman. " I can't wait any longer. I'll pay him for you when I return."

Raising himself on tiptoe, Dessouki began to handle the ropes, while Abou Nawass stood up to push off from the bank with the help of a long pole.

The felucca moved away, rocking gently, and left the row of other vessels. Suddenly cries were heard. Okkasionne had appeared at the top of the steps.

" Ahoy there! " he yelled. " Wait; you must wait for me."

With the monkey's arms round his neck he rushed down the steps, protesting and waving his arms.

" Hi, you there," he went on shouting in the direction of the boat while Mangua, her fur standing on end, clung despairingly to her master.

As he ran down the white stairs he resembled in turns some huge spider, a weird bird, a wind-blown tree, a sorcerer, and a phantom with a thousand arms! The woman, frightened by all these trans-formations, drew back and stood as near as possible to the boatman.

When he reached the bank the busker took off his sandals, and holding them in his hand plunged up to his knees in the water. Then clutching on to the felucca, he clambered on board under the indifferent eye of Abou Nawass. Then he sank down out of breath, squatting at the old woman's feet.

" Om Hassan! " he said to her, looking at her reproachfully, " I would never have believed this of you."

" Be quiet," said the boatman. " It's your fault. We couldn't wait until morning."

The old woman hastily emptied part of her money into the busker's outstretched hands, in the hope that he would quickly get off again. But the sailing-boat had already reached the middle of the river; it would take a little time to turn her round and return. Without saying another word the woman turned her back and went slowly towards the child's hiding-place.

Seated very close to Hassan she made no move-ment, said nothing which could allow his presence to be guessed at. But she picked up an end of her long veil and let it slip over the edge and hang down to the bottom of the trench among the bales. Merely by feeling the veil the child would know she had returned.

" Now, Abou Nawass, put me on shore," said the busker.

" I've lost too much time already," he replied. " Either you swim to the bank or you stay with us."

" Swim? I don't know how to swim! I'm only accustomed to dry land. Water and air aren't made to my measure."

" Then you've no choice; you stay."

Crouched down on her haunches, Saddika heard all they said, and cursed the boatman's obstinacy. She drove her nails into one of the sacks, making the fibre of the jute crack, digging into it until she felt the spongy cotton beneath her fingers.

Okkasionne threw a woebegone glance towards the bank and higher up at the vanishing town. Not knowing against whom to vent his rage— the boatman's calm demeanour disarmed him—he seized Mangua, unhooked her from his neck and thrust her into the bottom of his bag, closing it up by pulling on the cord and knotting it.

A barge going in the direction of the embankment—her two sails crossed in an X, full of jars and pottery—brushed against the felucca of Abou Nawass. The old woman hoped at one moment that the busker would leap across from one boat to the other. He did nothing. He seemed to be trying to ingratiate himself with the boatman by taking part in his mishap. But the latter, looking far into the distance over the gently raised prow, only seemed to be interested in the currents and the caprices of the breeze.

" Why worry? " the busker said to himself. " I'm a free man with nothing to keep me in any one place. Here, there, it's all the same! Go on, boatman, let's take the wind by the horns and slip away to the sea."

Since Abou Nawass made no reply, he addressed the monkey in a loud voice:

" A little journey will cheer us up, Mangua."

It was only then that he remembered having imprisoned the animal. He lifted up his bag and softly patted her, but the wistiti did not stir.

" Hullo! Ho! Mangua—my monkey! "

Filled with anxiety, he undid the cord and pulled the little beast out of the bag. Her body was limp and she seemed half suffocated. Trembling, Okkasionne put her down on the seat, and under Om Hassan's astonished gaze be began to let out piercing cries, ululating like a hired mourner did, hitting his cheeks and tearing at his clothes:

" Oh, Mangua! My beauty! My innocent one! "

With starting eyes, the busker shook his monkey, pulled her tail, massaged her back and the nape of her neck, pinched her ears, without any result. In the end, taking her between his two hands, and glueing his lips to hers, he began to breathe into the animal's mouth:

" Don't leave me, my daughter," he entreated, with tears in his voice.

Mangua blinked her eyelids, shut her mouth, shook her head. Then all at once she was on her feet and beginning to gambol again. Broken with emotion, Okkasionne lowered himself on to the deck and watched the monkey delightedly.

" What would become of Okkasionne without Mangua? " he exclaimed clapping his hands together. " You rogue! You pretended to be dead to frighten me—you rogue! You maniac! "

The boatman gave a slight smile.

" How many monkeys' lives are worth the life of a child? " wondered Om Hassan. She asked herself if God used this kind of measurement.

CHAPTER 2

The Nile glistened like the back of a fish, spread itself out, flowed far away from the city. A few houseboats tossed about on the surface, occasionally on one of their landing-stages a dim orange light twinkled.

The boatman was not talkative, Dessouki slept and Okkasionne prepared himself for sleep. A great peace settled all round them. The woman felt reassured; would her anguish vanish with the town? Beyond her, only long stretches of water lay ahead; beyond that water was still more water, and so on as far as the sea.

One more day, one more night and the child would rise up out of the shadow. From now until then she had only to keep all danger at a distance, to foresee every threat, to keep watch as the she-wolves did, with eyes that bored into the night. She had only to keep awake.

Om Hassan thought of Saïd; had he found rest tonight? She thought of her village, Barwat. Had they buried their dead in their hearts and had they found rest tonight? Rest. What did it mean to rest? Even later on when the child should have recovered, she would not find it any more. Had she ever known it? " I am not made for rest." Something was always exercising her mind, ceaselessly urging her on. Something she could not name and which no doubt resembled the mystery of life.

An hour went slowly by. Lulled by the swishing of the river, his eyes raised to the black vault pierced with stars, Okkasionne, allowed himself to be overcome by a feeling of beatitude.

Great layers of fatigue weighed down on Om Hassan's shoulders, rounding her back, tearing at the nape of her neck. Her head fell several times on to her chest, she straightened it time and again. Very soon, giving up all resistance, the old woman sank into sleep.

*
* *

The busker magnanimously, let loose his monkey. " Go along, my ferret! I'm setting you free! I'm not worried," he added for the benefit of the boatman. " She's too sensible to lean over the water." But Mangua, in spite of his encouragement, did not move.

" Come along, make the most of it; I want to see if you know how to behave yourself all on your own. Take a stroll. This space is made for your amusement. It's neither too high nor too large. Just the right size for you to make use of your freedom without losing it. The boat is yours and the little piece of sky above. See how it goes; it's never the same. With each movement of the vessel we're somewhere else. On another part of the water, under another bit of sky."

The monkey went off, retraced its steps, went away again.

"Everything is moving, boatman, even our dirty footprints. But what's at the bottom of it all? Emptiness? Then who knows anything about it? But that doesn't prevent everything going along and ourselves going along with the rest of it as well. Where to? I don't know at all! But we're going, that's certain. Like the water, the wind and the stars."

"It's true," said the boatman at last. "A calm night makes one think of strange things."

Climbing over the sacks, Mangua was amusing herself, scratching the jute and pulling out threads which she rubbed between her teeth. Then she advanced on all fours, snuffling in corners.

"Why have you chosen to live on the water, boatman?"

He waited, but the other said nothing.

"If I had the choice, I'd still prefer the land. Do you know that even if I had to choose between earth and sky, I'd still choose the earth? I like something you can feel, something you can find again, something which doesn't run away through your fingers. I like a hookah, black tea, love ... the sort that doesn't cling to your coat-tails. I like money to spend all at once. I like Mangua to be dressed like a princess, and wearing rich stuff fit for a king myself; even if next day I haven't got enough to buy an olive to eat. Recently I've put through a splendid deal. I was clever enough to discover one of the last cases of cholera. Do you

know that I was paid for this? Royally rewarded.
Well! Boatman, are you listening to me? Why
do you turn your head away? In my opinion it's
a good deed. I denounce a dying man in order to
save the sound ones. Don't you think it's a wise
precaution? My conscience is clear."

"Then stop excusing yourself," said the boatman.

"I'm not excusing myself, I'm explaining. If
I'd thought of it sooner, the town would have
counted me among its benefactors. They would
one day have set up a bronze statue of me and I
would have insisted on their sculpting Mangua at
my side. Eh, why don't you answer?"

Jumping from sack to sack, the monkey had
arrived near the sleeping old woman. With velvety
footsteps she crept round her, then sat down beside
her and pretended to be asleep like her. At last,
tired of this mimicry, she began to ferret and sniff
around again. In a few seconds she had discovered
the hiding-place. She leant over, stretched her
hairy arm into the hollow, tapped against the inner
surface, touched the motionless child. Jumping
up and down, she raised both hands at once and
let out strident cries to alert her master.

Om Hassan awoke with a start, sensing danger;
she seized the monkey by the scruff of the neck and
sent her rolling to the end of the boat.

"How dare you raise your hand against Mangua?"
cried the busker.

He unhooked a lantern, took it down, and
walked threateningly towards the place where the

woman was standing. Hoisting himself up on to
the bales of cotton, he soon came face to face with
her. But suddenly noticing the trench, he pushed
Om Hassan sharply back, took a few more steps
and held his light over the bottom of the nook.
At the sight of that bluish body, drowned in the
beams of light, he remained frozen to the spot, his
mouth open, his eyes starting from their sockets.
All at once he began to yell:

" It's the cholera! The cholera! "

Turning back, he ran towards the boatman and
ordered him to put to shore immediately. He waved
his lantern about so much that Dessouki, fearing he
might set fire to the ship, quickly took it from him,
still rubbing his eyes with the other hand.

" Death is with us, boatman. Let's return
quickly."

" Death is always with us," said Abou Nawass.

" Be quick, boatman, there's no time for argu-
ing."

" Stop moving about and leave that woman to
her child," replied the other.

" You're mad too! You're mad! "

Perceiving that his words made no impression
but merely spent themselves against a wall of indifference, the busker turned to the woman and
called her a " criminal " and " crazy ".

The old woman stood up in front of the trench,
making a screen for Hassan with her body. Then,
fearful that all those cries would reach and terrify
the child, she started walking towards the busker,
descending from the platform and advancing along

a little lane bordered by the sacks. The violence of her feeling deformed her features, masked her face:

" Clear off," she hissed between her teeth.

Okkasionne took a step backwards, but the woman still came on. Soon she was so close he could feel her hot breath against his cheeks.

" I swear it, I'll tear out your guts, if you don't shut up," she cried.

The busker stammered, retreated again.

" Another word, one single word, and I'll throw you into the water! "

With her veils inflated by the wind, Om Hassan appeared to tower over Okkasionne, terrifying him, a head taller than him, to come straight out of a nightmare. Throwing himself on all fours, the busker took refuge near the seat, leant his back against it and shut his eyes so as not to see anything any more. Mangua had just jumped on to his knees, and curled up one against the other they looked like a heap of stones.

" Life's a calamity," fumed the busker into his monkey's ear. " A real calamity."

The woman went slowly back to her place. Then she sat down on the other side of the trench, facing the man with the monkey. She never took her implacable eyes from his face. Neither he nor the monkey dared raise their heads the whole of that night.

The young Nubian, who understood nothing of what had happened, mumbled prayers in a corner.

Abou Nawass, looking into the distance, had begun to sing again:

" I sing for the moon
And the moon for the bird
The bird for the sky
And then the sky for the water
The water sings for the boat
The boat for my voice
My voice for the moon
So it begins again.

On the land and in the water
My song will be lost
Where the dark is so high
My song is blotted out.

The moon heard me
And through the moon, the bird,
The sky heard me
And through the sky, the water,
The boat heard me
And through the boat, my voice,
My voice heard me
And I hear my voice."

Time went by; then the dawn streaked the
horizon. A pale-coloured sky hung over the river
and its banks.

CHAPTER 3

ONE could see far into the distance because of the clear, dry morning and the flatness of the country. Sometimes it seemed like a film of green laid over a vast expanse. The river contracted, squeezed itself between banks shaped like the backs of tortoises, covered with sand or gravel. When the sun at its fullest and highest ravaged the countryside all round, the sight of weeping-willows or mastic-trees made one imagine the shelter of their branches, forming cages of shade by the side of the water.

During this one night the busker had aged by several years. Crouching with his elbows on his knees, his hands pressed against his cheeks, he tilted his head from one side to the other, whimpering. The monkey sat motionless by his side, blinking her eyes without stopping.

Towards daybreak, Abou Nawass had relinquished the helm to the young Nubian and gone to sleep.

Om Hassan knew she had nothing more to fear from the busker, she had kept her eyes on him all night; he appeared to be prostrated, beaten, unresponsive. She got up, and turning round took a few steps to the side to look at the sun. The sun would reach its apex, decline, disappear and then be born again. At the next sunrise the child would have defeated death.

During that last day she must prevent herself from disturbing him, avoid any attentions which would cause him a useless effort. Perhaps she should even look at him as little as possible, so as not to force him to respond. She would refuse to allow herself to be anxious because of the risk of communicating her anxiety. Hassan must be wholly imbued with his coming metamorphosis, nothing must be allowed to interrupt the dark and slow working of his whole body.

Thus she prowled for a long time round the recumbent child. A piece of cloth fixed over the shelter completely disguised it.

But at the end of an hour, overcome with impatience, she stooped down, and lying on the sacks raised a corner of the cloth. " Only for a second," she said to herself, " just to see."

In spite of her resolutions, at the sight of Hassan she was plunged in deep terror. His limbs were contracted, moist, covered with cold sweat as with a second skin. A stale, sickening smell rose up from the nook. The child's tunic was covered with urine stains. Saddika was tempted to take it off him, wash it, dry it in the sun and then to put it on him again, clean and tidy. But she soon gave up the idea; the effort the child made to breathe already seemed beyond his strength. She could not ask anything more of him. It seemed as though he had an engine inside his body which he forced himself to keep running and which the least distraction would stop.

Om Hassan's eyes filled with tears. She quickly

thrust herself backwards so that the child should not discover she was crying. In spite of his quiet face and sluggish gaze, she always had the impression that nothing escaped Hassan.

With the cloth restored to its place and the child sheltered once more, Saddika struggled with herself; but in vain. Every hour that passed weighed cruelly on her heart. " I am too old, too old," she moaned. " I can't do anything for him." Never before had her mind been so disordered. Raising her head towards the arid sky, marbled like an empty shell, she was shaken with violent sobbing. Dessouki, who could see her back, guessed by the heaving of her shoulders that she was in tears. He clicked his tongue several times against the roof of his mouth, not knowing any more what to think of all this business.

Saddika, letting her tears flow, let loose a torrent within her which could not be dammed up any longer. Was this she, the same woman who had walked so far, searched so much, mastered her despair and fear? Was it she who had endured being chained to the man with the monkey? Were these the same legs which afterwards had carried her through the town, and climbed those innumerable steps? Were these the same arms which had pushed the cart, supported and carried the child?

She bowed her head under the weight of these memories. She was assailed and overwhelmed by nightmares; she no longer resisted them.

*

*   *

Hassan is as heavy as two children put together, then as heavy as three, then eight. . . . He weighs as much as a hundred children! The woman walks relentlessly along a stony road without end, each step seems like an eternity. She doubles up, falls to the ground, her old body goes on one knee and then the other, always carrying the child in her outstretched arms. Right at the end there is a vague mass, a rock no doubt. Is she going towards that block of granite? Nevertheless she continues to advance; she keeps going. But all at once she sinks down. The child turns round, grips on to her shoulders, climbs on to her back and lies there; his cold breath freezes her ear, he whispers to her never to stop. She goes forward, but she is crawling now, helping herself along with her hands, and the child weighs heavily on her shoulder-blades, on her loins. . . . She must at all costs go forward, escape from this road, free herself from this shattering load, get rid of these stones which tear at her hands and belly, flee from this treeless path, this merciless sun. A sound of water in the distance. . . . Is there a spring yonder, in that granite rock? Is it a mirage? What does it signify?

At the same moment, other springs began to flow. Transported by her nightmares, Om Hassan was sitting on the sacks not far from the child, weeping ceaselessly. Her eyes overflowed. Her swarthy, wrinkled cheeks were drowned in tears. She let herself go. She allowed herself to be overwhelmed and did not even raise her arm to wipe her drenched face with the back of her hand. Her tears slid past the corners of her mouth, ran down the length of her neck, wet the opening of her dress. How many centuries was it since Saddika had wept?

*

*   *

A village. . . . This might have happened today, yesterday, in a bygone age. . . . A country road, white with dust, no one in sight. Saddika puts down her doll and goes to paddle in the canal. Suddenly a cart dragged along by an infuriated mule emerges on to the road. The wheels turn rapidly, madly, with a creaking sound. Before Saddika can climb up the slope again, the cart sweeps round, bowls along, passes her, has passed by. . . . There is nothing left on the ground but a few rags, a little straw and some tiny splinters.

"I will make you another one," says Nabila, her elder sister.

"Never, never. . . . This is the doll I want."

"I'll make you another just like it, with these same rags, this same straw, these same sticks."

"No, no. . . . I want mine."

With nothing but this little heap of mud and stuff in her hands, Saddika sobs. She will never be comforted.

However, by the middle of the night she has already come to the end of her tears. Astonished and disappointed that her tears should so soon be used up, she returns to the canal and ceremoniously lays the remains of her doll on the water.

It floats away, rolled up in a damp winding-sheet, an eternity of tears will envelop it for ever. . . .

And then Saddika is weeping again, and this makes a chaplet of tears linking her with the present. Her father is beating her because she refuses the man he has chosen for her. The room is a dark den. Her father's worn face is consumed by fatigue but he knows how to strike her! Her mother sits huddled against the wall, echoing everything he says. With her head buried in her arms and her elbows raised, Saddika receives the blows but she knows that she will not give in. Although her father is now threatening her with his hoe, her mother trembling in a corner, the neighbours and the fiancé awaiting an answer, she will not give in. She does not weep now, in front of her father who is beating her. She will weep tonight, cowering in the dark, thinking of Saïd whom she loves.

*

* *

You shape your life. You must have the will to live. The will to live and love is a natural, vigorous tree growing inside your body. Life is what it is. Men are what they are. The best is always somewhere. In sand, in granite, in lead, in ourselves. The gift of tears, the grace of tears is always somewhere to be found.

How aware was she of her old body, how conscious she was of her old spirit, all moulded by the past! How everything stirred within her! A thousand lives contradicted each other within her single life. She had the spirit to renounce and the spirit to continue; a soul for every day and one for looking into the distance. A soul full of anger and also one imbued with the most secret tenderness.

After one has wept for a long time there is peace. Om Hassan wiped her face, pressing the palms of her hands over her eyes and then parting them like wings towards her temples. Before leaning over the child once more she removed all traces of weeping. She even hid a lock of white hair under her veil. Hassan would undoubtedly be upset, he had never seen his grandmother with her hair uncovered. Still seated, she turned towards the hiding-place.

Once more she lifted the cloth which covered the recess. Nothing had changed, yet everything was different.

The mottled skin, the sweat were like borrowed clothing. That burning breath did not signify the end but was a sign of a great struggle, and nothing was gained without a struggle. This flesh, this collection of bones, was not really Hassan. Hassan was behind it all, keeping watch. The child himself did not seem to believe in his own body. In spite of his body he was going to live. Human children performed these miracles, not dolls. Didn't he ask her yesterday: "Are we leaving?" He knew they were going towards the sea. He wanted to see the sea. He would see it.

A great wind blew away uncertainties and sad memories. Her mother was no longer there, standing abashed against the wall; her mother was singing at twilight while the men returned from the fields, and her father had just bought his first feddan.

It was the moonlit evening when Saïd loved her. There was the cotton-gathering, when she was six years old, stooping under the blazing sun, there were the fields, so freshly green that one could wish to climb to the top of a tree and then dive down into that green sea. There was the city with its beating pulse. There was tomorrow " and that child that I shall have made," the child who would make things in his turn. There was this river, this beautiful earth, the strange mildness of the mornings. There were the banks, the life which sprang up everywhere, those women who came down carrying their jars and their linen. There was the end of the cholera, the end of evil. The cholera condemned, buried, altogether dead in the body of this child.

CHAPTER 4

TURNING his back on the felucca, Okkasionne looked at the shore where people were beginning to appear. They were near, very near, but nevertheless out of reach. "This is the ship of death, and not one of those who come and go so calmly on the banks are aware of it," he grumbled.

They were all in serious danger, those on board and also those on shore. If the woman took it into her head to wash the child's dirty clothes, the river would be the cause of further deaths. "Crass ignorance. These women from the country are rotten with prejudice." The busker flattered himself that he was a townsman. His family had been established in the city for three generations; his father still kept a shop there. But Okkasionne could not bear to stay behind a counter. He lived according to his fancy. Away from restrictions, beyond walls. . . . But now he who had devoted his life to fantasy found himself on this boat, in a limited space, encircled by wood and water, a prisoner of human stupidity. This woman was a pest. She was as narrow-minded as the other peasants, she and those of her sort had never really risen up out of the soil. What was the use of their lives? You asked yourself sometimes. . . . The busker reproached himself above all for having lacked perception. He had let himself be carried away by fellow feeling, by generosity. See how he had been rewarded! "I prided myself that I knew about life, people ... I have much left to learn." Om Hassan was practically a murderess. Could he have suspected it? Yesterday hadn't she threatened to throw him into the water? The memory of that scene made him shiver. And then she had watched over the child all night like a wounded animal. Given the chance she would have pounced savagely on top of death itself, without fear, with her teeth, with her nails. ... Okkasionne shrugged his shoulders: " With people of this sort we'll never get out of the mess we're in. ... After all, I don't care. Life's a tight-rope, a mad balancing act. You must just swing from one foot to the other. It's not worth while taking too much notice of what goes on round you, otherwise beware of a fall! You'll perish before your hour has struck. ..." However, he considered he couldn't forgive himself for having been so dense, and for having fallen so low in one night. Hadn't he passed that night, huddled up in the bottom of the boat like a lamb waiting to be sheared? He felt ashamed of his cowardice and turned round to look the woman in the face.

She was no longer worrying about him. Stretched out on the sacks, with her head under the stuff which screened the recess, she was talking in a low voice to the child. You could hear her voice, slightly singing, but only scraps of sentences from that monotonous, rhythmical flow reached the man with the monkey.

What was she plotting now, and why didn't she let that unfortunate child die in peace? One word came across, then another, the busker heard " young." Then he heard " parasol . . ." Then " dragon-fly, corn, stars, house, hunger," floated to the end of the ship.

*
* *

" The river is so narrow this morning, my son," murmured the old woman, bent over the child; " you can see everything that happens on the banks, as though you were there. . . . The sun is bright, you don't see it behind your veil, but tomorrow you'll look it full in the face. . . . The fields have never seemed to me so new, nor such a fresh green. There's a road a little higher up between the eucalyptus-trees. You can see a lorry going along it, silver-coloured as you like them, with double tyres. After that comes a row of camels. Wait while I count them. . . . There are five. But the fifth is small and puny, he has weak knees. One day you'll take me to visit the pyramids, on the back of a camel. . . ."

She went on:

" Do you know what I see now ? A big man sitting on a little trotting donkey. The man is as fat as Fikhry the dyer. He's wearing new, orange-coloured Turkish slippers with their points turned outwards so that everyone can admire them as he passes by. He is holding a white parasol lined with green which casts a beautiful shadow wherever he goes! We'll buy ourselves a parasol like that,

so that we can walk about under our own shade. . . .
There are children on the bank sprinkling a sheet
of dragon-flies with water. You know those insects
which only live for one day? If only I had one grain
of corn in my pocket! Only one seed! I would
have cast it here, on the edge of the black, fertile
earth, so that at the end of ten years, when we came
back, you and I, we would recognise the place we
had passed. . . . Hassan, how right you are to want
to build houses when you grow up, that's what is
lacking in our countryside. Houses like those in
the town but white, all white, inside which everyone
would eat enough to satisfy their hunger. . . ."

*

* *

" Hunger," Okkasionne heard her say.   " I'm
hungry too." He searched in the bottom of his
bag and found nothing there. Then turning to
Dessouki, who was at the helm, the busker put his
hand several times up to his mouth, to show that he
wanted to eat. The Nubian bent down, moved a
board under his seat, slipped his hand into the
opening and brought out some bread and onions.

" Take this," he said to him.

First Okkasionne made sure that the woman had
not been near the food.

" She has her own provisions," replied the other.

The busker broke the flat, round loaf in two,
then dug his teeth into the first half and tore out a
great mouthful which he began slowly chewing,
changing it from one cheek to the other. But at the

thought of the epidemic and of the child being so near, his gorge rose and Okkasionne could not swallow anything. He got up and spat into the river.

" Here," he said to the monkey, handing her the rest, " You try. . . ."

Mangua imitated her master, and thinking it was a game, overdid her grimaces. So the busker took the last piece out of her hands and would have thrown it all overboard, but the young Nubian leapt from his place and seized his arm as it swung in the air. Without a word he took back the rest of the loaf and replaced it in the store.

*

* *

For fear of the sailing-boat running on to the sand, Abou Nawass pushed away from the banks on either side with a long pole which he plunged into the silt. Standing up on the prow he came and went along the edge of the boat. His legs were brown and muscular, his feet stood firm on the narrowest surface. He passed several times in silence beside the place where Om Hassan was crouching. At last, as all danger seemed to have receded, he stopped for a few minutes beside the trench.

" Is the child better ? " he inquired.

" He will live," replied the old woman. " He will live, I tell you."

" If you say so, it must be true," the man replied.

Holding his long pole between his folded arms, he remained there for a long moment, silent and attentive, facing the old woman. Then he went away.

Taking up his position at the extreme point of the prow, he now gazed at the course of the water. The corpse of an animal swollen like a water-skin, floating on the surface of the river, another sailing-boat coming into sight, were all possible obstacles which still needed taking care of between these narrow banks.

*

*   *

Huddled up with Mangua crouching on his knees, Okkasionne had seen the old people talking together. What had they said to each other? The boatman had gone away again; he seemed solely preoccupied with the fate of his boat. He was a man without imagination. A man without a future or a past. He could have been born at any time, anywhere, a boat and a river were all he needed to begin sailing again, without worrying about his surroundings. As for the old woman, she was a poor lunatic but a dangerous one. In this country the women become obstinate with age. " Mad, criminal, ignorant." All the same he could not help admiring her performance. She probably had not slept for days, and she still found the strength to invent stories for the child. As though he could hear them! It was impossible to communicate anything to Om Hassan or the boatman. Funny people, they live elsewhere, in their own worlds! Dessouki, perhaps?

" Do you know that that woman is making us

run the gravest risks?" said Okkasionne, approaching the young Nubian and speaking to him in a low voice. "I've seen the child. He'll croak. It's written all over his face. There's nothing to be done about it. Few of them recover, and as for him, I tell you, he's already as good as dead."

"Do you really think he'll die? The woman says that on the sixth day—"

"The sixth day wasn't made for that poor wretch, I swear it to you! Look here, if I took you to the fish market and showed you the sacks full of fish, you'd be able to pick out the rotten ones, wouldn't you?"

"I don't know anything about fish."

"After all these weeks on the water, have you never fished?"

"Never."

"How's that?"

"Among us boatmen, there are those who fish and those who carry the freight."

"But you have plenty of time to do both."

"Time's what it is."

"You evidently lack enterprise; you're content with very little."

"Each one to his trade."

"If I were a boatman I would do both."

"That remains to be seen."

"But I tell you so."

"What are you trying to get at with your stories of fish?"

"I was explaining to you that from what I've seen of men I can tell when one of them's going to croak. I have the flair, I sense it. I've never been mistaken. When I tell you the child's going to croak, it's the truth. Do you want me to say that the child is death itself? Look how he does nothing; lets himself go. It's the old woman who moves about. She's alive, not he."

" Perhaps she has enough life for two and will give him— "

" I know what you mean but such things can't be handed on."

" And suppose that for once the contrary were to happen? "

" Listen, it's no use. If a thing's impossible, there's nothing you can do. Even God can do nothing. Why are you so obstinate, too? The only reasonable thing left to do is to save our own skins. In a few hours' time they won't be worth much. But there's one chance for us, and we must take it! "

" Which chance? " asked the Nubian.

" You're steering; run us into a sandbank. As soon as we touch the shore, you and I will escape. You're a sharp lad; I'll find you a bread-winning job in the city."

Dessouki turned his head away without answering.

" I tell you the air is infected here. In a few hours it will be too late for us too. You're young; don't forget you only have one life."

" And what then? Do you cling to life so much? What do you get out of life? "

" In life there's life," said the busker.

" Yesterday you were complaining," the other reminded him. " I heard you say ' life is a calamity'."

" Yesterday's not today."

The Nubian shrugged his shoulders.

" Then answer me, what are you going to do? "

" You can count me out— " He was silent and then continued, " There was a time when I had a mother." Then noticing the busker's ironic grimace, he turned his face away again.

*
*   *

Hassan was not, in fact, getting better. He couldn't hear the old woman's words any longer. He breathed with great difficulty. Saddika was afraid that he would not be able to keep up the effort much longer. She went to fetch one of the palm-branches which covered the jar of water and returned to fan the child.

The hours passed slowly. Om Hassan's heart leapt as though it were trying to escape from this motionless time.

A bit farther on she caught sight of some women gathered at the edge of the bank. You could hear their shrill voices with their occasional tender or childish inflections. Surrounded with metal pots which sparkled in the sun, they washed their linen on flat stones, while others, carrying their jars pressed against their hips, came down to join them. Saddika suddenly saw herself among them as though time had ceased to exist. That was she in her bright dress, that young girl sitting surrounded by her companions in black.

" Then it's true you're getting married, Saddika ? "

There is a burst of laughter. One of the women tweaks the end of her plaited hair. Saddika stays crouching, her elbows on her knees, her face between her hands; she is the only one who does not laugh. She gazes at the sailing-boat. Yes, it is she who goes by, accompanied by a child she does not yet know.

" Where are you going, old woman ? " called one of the peasant women.

" I'm going to my village," replied Om Hassan.

" What is your village called ? "

" Barwat," she said, still fanning the child.

" The cholera is at Barwat," cried another.

" No, the cholera is over," replied her companion.

The young girl in red was she herself, Saddika. She recognised the dress, she recognised herself ; she was silent, as though she already bore the weight of all this. She remained seated while all the others ran towards the water to make themselves heard.

" Where have you come from ? " called one of the women, cupping her hands to her mouth.

" From Cairo— " replied the old woman.

" Are there many dead there ? "

" No, not many— "

One of them, standing a little apart, snatched up the child who was splashing about beside her, and held it up at arm's length so that everyone could see it:

" Look, old woman, this one has had the cholera but he has recovered."

The child flung himself about, kicked his legs, impatient to get back to the sand.

" They brought him back from the hospital ten days ago. He's more beautiful than before."

The words echoed, Saddika contemplated the scene; Okkasionne observed the wriggling child with its round belly.

The mother's sleeves slipped down and you could see her bare arms, humid and brown, of the same swarthy colour as the child's body. The boat glided away, the scene vanished. The young girl was no more than a scarlet dot.

Saddika went on fanning Hassan; he breathed harder and harder, there was a forge in his chest.

Farther on a woman was carrying a tiny child astride her shoulder, her linen on the other arm, and there were five other children round her who worried her with their squealing. She needed a hundred arms to deal with that swarm of brats. Seeing the boat and the old woman sitting there, she could not help shouting :

" I wish old age would come quickly so that I could go for a trip like you! "

The banks receded, soon they would no longer be a part of the journey. Om Hassan would find she was even more alone than in the morning. How would she get through this last night? What would she look at in the darkness which was about to descend? The boatman would no doubt have nothing more to say; he had gone back to his tiller.

The young Nubian would be ceaselessly busy. There would only be the man with the monkey.

The woman sought him with her eyes. At that moment, with his monkey wedged between his knees, he was trying to smooth its fur with a metal comb. She would have liked to talk to him, but how was it to be done?

CHAPTER 5

NIGHT had absorbed everything. The boat was
alone in the world. Beside the yellow wall of the
school, the *oustaz* Selim had said: " On the sixth
day there is a veritable resurrection." He did not
say it for himself because he was dead. He said it
for the child. The young teacher was dead. Why
did good people die? Why? It was better not to
think too much about it tonight. One must not
think about several things at the same time. It was
enough to think of the child. She must only think
about the child.

A little conversation would help the hours slip
by. A fairly strong wind had risen, the boatman and
his mate were shortening the sails. Om Hassan
gazed once again at the busker. Their eyes met. He
was also longing to talk. Should she call him? She
hesitated, then with a movement of her arm she
made a sign to him to approach. He was disconcerted and looked all around him. No, it must be
meant for him. He fastened his monkey to the chain
and attached it to the leg of the seat.

" Me? " he asked, as soon as he was on his feet.

She repeated the same gesture. Because of the
darkness he could hardly see her face, but suddenly
remembering her threats of the evening before, her
distorted features, her burning breath against his

cheeks, he was seized with panic and sat down again.

" Come here," she said. " Don't be afraid."

He got up, advanced a few steps, gradually recovered his self-assurance and at last, scrambling up on to the sacks, slowly approached.

" Can't you get to sleep? " asked Saddika when he was quite close.

" No, I haven't even closed my eyes."

" Nor have I."

" That I can understand."

He had discarded his cap and cloak, the wind blew his narrow tunic against his chest, on to his hips. He looked thin and miserable. A butterfly without wings.

" Sit down," motioned the woman.

Okkasionne sat down opposite, on the other side of the trench. They were silent. What should they say?

" How is the child? " asked the busker at last.

" It's his last night," said the woman.

" His last night? "

" His last night of suffering, you understand; he's on the way to recovery."

" Do you think so? " he let out.

" I'm certain of it."

Her tone admitted of no reply. At the other end of the boat Mangua was pulling on her chain.

" Mangua, if you keep that up," the busker called to her, relieved by the distraction, " I'll throw you to the fishes! "

Another silence. A dragging ball-and-chain of

silence. This time the woman took up the conversation:

" What happened to your monkey yesterday? "

" The madcap tried to suffocate herself! "

" What wouldn't I do to save Mangua? " he suddenly asked himself. Then he brushed the absurd idea away. What was the use of cudgelling his head with suppositions? Nothing is foreseeable. Nothing is ever the same. Yesterday, could he have imagined it possible that he would be sitting quietly beside a case of cholera? Time, boredom, circumstances, wear away fear and make you into another man.

The night stagnated and then somersaulted forward again with each exchange of words. Okkasionne avoided speaking of the child, but he questioned the woman about Saïd, about the dyer, the blind man, and other people of their district. Om Hassan replied, remembered, told stories. She had nothing more to fear from the man, she even felt a certain sympathy for him. She went so far as to tell him about her journey to Barwat.

" Do you know the sea? " she finally asked him.

" I've seen the sea only once when I hid in a truck between two crates of oranges, to make the journey to Alexandria."

" And how many days does it take by sailing-boat? "

" I don't know. I don't think it takes very long."

" Good. I promised Hassan years ago I would show him the sea."

" No doubt I'm stupid," said the busker to

himself, " but this woman is stupidity itself. The child will never get as far as the sea. Perhaps not one of those on board this ship will get there either, and all because of this old woman." At this thought his anger returned, he stood up suddenly, turned his back on the woman, and went cursing to himself back to his place beside the monkey.

*

*　　*

Towards midnight, a sand-storm arose. The breeze lashed the water, ruffling it up in patches.

Dessouki was asleep in the stern, with his tunic pulled up and wrapped round his head. The boatman held the tiller; his distant gaze imposed silence, discouraged any intercourse. Okkasionne had not taken his eyes off the old woman, he noticed that she was trembling with fatigue.

Gathering up his blue cloak, which had fallen from his shoulders the evening before and slipped behind the seat, he went towards Om Hassan. She did not even hear him approach.

" Put this on, you're cold," he said, covering her with the starry material.

She still shivered.

" Come down under shelter; you're full in the wind here."

" No, I can't leave him. I ought to keep watch beside him."

" But he doesn't even see you."

" He feels I'm there."

" Do you think so ? "

" He knows I'm as near as possible. He knows it."

" Very well, I understand. . . ."

The busker went off to his seat again.

Huddled under the gleaming cloak, the woman looked older, more pitiful still. Okkasionne could not bear to see her thus. Unfastening his monkey and carrying it under his arm, he climbed up again to Om Hassan.

" If I may, I'll watch with you," he said, laying himself down at her feet.

She bowed her head:

" Heaven will reward you."

Fighting against sleep and still thinking of the woman, the man with the monkey asked himself whether so much obstinacy would not achieve its purpose.

CHAPTER 6

ALL through the long night the woman had kept watch without trying to look at the child. Now dawn was near.

Leaning over the side of the boat, she filled a can which Dessouki had lent her with water. Standing apart, she refreshed her arms, her neck, her face, wet her hair. The water was good. When she rinsed out her mouth, she was left with a taste of salt. " Life," she murmured, " life . . ." She was ready, she drew breath, she waited.

Okkasionne watched her out of the corner of his eye: " Old idiot," he muttered, with a sort of tenderness.

Om Hassan returned to her place, folded the huge cloak with measured movements, put it under the head of the recumbent busker.

" I wasn't asleep," he said.

Then she calmly went to sit down, facing the east, her hands clasped together. Every tree that went past, every stone, every grain of sand on the shore was drowned in the past, was dissolved for ever in oblivion. Never again would she remember all this; she would not want to remember it. You should not carry nightmares along with you, nor cover a child's footsteps with shadows.

The busker rubbed his eyes, scratched the soles

of his feet, sat up again. Was he right to wake up? Sleep was the only refuge left to him; what was there in store for him today? His tongue was dry, his head empty. Once he was on his feet again, he began prowling round Om Hassan, out of curiosity and impatience.

" Well? " he inquired.

The old woman's face was smooth, serene, happy.

" He has had a good night, I haven't heard him moaning."

" Perhaps because of the wind blowing— "

" I have no ear for the wind, I only have an ear for Hassan," she replied.

" Very well, old woman, I was only asking for information. So you say he didn't groan? "

" Not once. He'll soon be well."

" Soon? When is soon? "

" When the sun is risen."

" But it's already dawn, Om Hassan. If the child is going to recover, he is already recovered."

" We must wait until the sun is completely full."

How could he explain to her what she would not understand. " Never mind, let it pass, we shall see!" Okkasionne had only to be quiet, to wait at her side.

" Very well, we'll wait."

" We must wait," Saddika repeated.

The sun drew slowly out of the depths. The busker no longer knew what to hope for. For time to stand still or to roll on, taking them far from today, this week, this year? It would be better to make an end of it. He could see the sunrise on Om

Hassan's face. Little by little her dress, her hands, her chin, her cheeks, her face became tinged. Her whole face was lit up, blazed like the old copper pans beside the fire. Then the woman clapped her hands together and began to sing softly: " Sun which riseth up all rosy from over the rosy mountain! "

She said in a firm voice: " Now he is well."

Okkasionne was shaken by so much assurance, thinking, " Of the two of us, I am probably the most ignorant."

Saddika said to the boatman:

" Hassan is well again."

At the stern of the boat, Abou Nawass—who had changed his headgear and now wore a bluish turban —inclined his head several times to show he had fully understood.

Om Hassan showed no sign of impatience, she had no more need to look, nor to touch. But the busker could not keep still.

" Go and see," he said, " go and see . . ."

The old woman stood up, went towards him and placed her hand on his shoulder:

" Go yourself, Okkasionne, you shall be the one to give me the good news," she said, to set the seal on their reconciliation.

" Me? "

The busker was not expecting to be thus honoured, nor did he like the idea very much either. Casting an anxious glance towards the boatman and his mate, he longed to attract their attention, to ask them to come, to go and see with him. But neither of them were looking. Om Hassan's hand lay on his shoulder, constraining and tender.

" Yes, you! Go, my son— "

He still hesitated:

" But what must I do? "

" It's easy. You lift up the mosquito-net which I have put over his face, and you look. The other evening you saw death. This morning you will recognise life."

" And my monkey? What must I do with my monkey? " asked the busker, delaying the moment of execution.

" Leave her with me."

Then Okkasionne moved in the direction of the recess; but at each step he turned round anxiously, hoping she would call him back.

" You needn't be frightened," said Saddika, " I will be responsible." Then placing her left hand flat on her chest: " He is recovered, I tell you! "

" Very well. . . . I'm going."

Was he going to believe too? He knelt down near the trench. But at once he was seized with doubt. He lingered, scratched the edge of one of the sacks with his black nails, perspired in great drops, searched for the boatman with his eyes.

" Lean over," said the woman.

He stooped. Hassan was completely covered up. The piece of material disguised his body, and the grey square of cloth his face. Okkasionne put out his arm, reached slowly to the bottom of the hiding-place. At last, taking hold of the corner of the handkerchief between his thumb and forefinger, he prepared to raise it. For the last time, however, he hesitated, questioned the woman with his eyes.

" Take off that veil," she said, in the same tone.

There was nothing left for him to do but obey.

All was motionless. The countryside froze. Time stood still. The birds stopped flying. Even the lapping of the water was no longer heard.

Finally, with a rapid jerk—pulling the end of the mosquito-net towards him—the busker in a single movement unveiled the face of the child.

* * *

With the grey square fluttering at the ends of his fingers, Okkasionne drew back horrified as far as the middle of the boat. Then the handkerchief fell, and the busker looked at his own fingers in horror.

Om Hassan would have gone to him but her legs gave way. Everything became mixed up in her head, her words fell over one another, became entangled. Only inarticulate sounds came out of her mouth.

" Speak," she pronounced at last.

Okkasionne had no need to speak. " Poor madwoman," he murmured. With one bound the monkey had jumped from the old woman's arms into his; and now, both together, they let out those ululations which accompany the dead.

Om Hassan took an eternity to cross the small space which separated her from the recess, while the others watched her. Clouds gathered before her eyes. It was grey, black; her body was being sucked down to the bottom of a well. It was grey again. At the end of an infinitely long passage, tangled with spiders' webs, she saw a faint light which she tried to reach. She stretched both arms towards it. She would never reach it.

Leaving the tiller in the Nubian's hands, the boatman ran forward; but he was too late, the old woman had collapsed. The shock made a dull thud which sharply interrupted the busker's wailing. Thrusting aside Mangua, who was clinging to his tunic, Okkasionne went up to the old woman, fallen full-length on her back, while Abou Nawass moved quickly towards the child.

The busker knelt behind Om Hassan, slid forward, supported her head, raised her up, rested her on his folded knees. Then he stroked her moist temples, gently patted her wrinkled cheeks; but he felt sure the woman had died of the death of the child. He must not even hope any longer that she would live. Never had the busker felt so much grief. One day you fall off your rope, you lose your balance. You find yourself back again among the others, amidst other people's suffering, you don't play any longer. You can't go on playing any more. " My heart is bleeding, for the first time."

Accustomed to pierce the distances, Abou Nawass was searching with his grey eyes in the bottom of the recess for the unknown child. He slipped his arm into the darkest part, reached down until his hand touched the body. The forehead was motionless. He felt the arms, the wrists where no pulse beat. He lingered over the chest, touched the stomach, pressed the thighs and knees. All was hard, cold, with the cold of caves. Could this shape, this icy stone, be a child?

" Om Hassan," he shouted suddenly, guessing that the old woman had no more than a few seconds to live. " You are the one who's right, the child is alive! "

This shape, this stone, this icy rock—certainly a child was very different from this. The boatman raised his voice:

" The child is alive! " he proclaimed.

And Dessouki at the helm took up the refrain:

" Om Hassan, the child is alive! "

Disconcerted, the busker turned from one to the other, trying to understand. " Okkasionne, you're the one to tell me the good news," she had said to him.

" His cheeks are getting warm," continued the boatman. " Hassan has just caught my finger in his little hand—and he holds it! If you knew how firmly he holds it, Om Hassan! "

Never had Abou Nawass felt so intensely what a child was. " He is alive," he repeated to himself. " Tomorrow is alive."

" His strength has returned," cried the Nubian, whose face was aglow, "he grips the boatman's finger in his little hand."

Still stroking the old woman's face, the busker sadly shook his head. She was already too far gone, she did not hear their calling. " You shall be the one to tell me the good news, Okkasionne," she had said to him.

" Everything will go on as before," the boatman went on. " I have told Hassan we are going as far as the sea, and he has understood me! "

And the young Nubian who had never seen the child's face and did not know what he looked like when he was standing up suddenly began to see him. Never had he been so much alive!

" Hassan understands that we're going towards the sea! " he repeated as loudly as possible.

Okkasionne stooped, gently turned Saddika's face to one side, put his lips to her ear and repeated after the others:

" You were right, Om Hassan, your child is alive— " he paused after each sentence so that the words had time to penetrate. " His cheeks are getting warm. He is holding the boatman's finger firmly in his little hand. Everything is going on as before, Om Hassan. We are going to the sea."

On the bank a naked, solitary, little boy was collecting water in his cupped hands and emptying it into the bottom of a hole he had dug in the sand.

A bird with a white breast and wings of steel— like those one sees out at sea—skimmed over the mast and then vanished at a dizzy speed.

" You've given him your last breath, Om Hassan," yelled the boatman.

" You've given him your last breath and he is alive! " announced Dessouki.

" You've saved him with your last breath," murmured Okkasionne, his lips brushing the old woman's face.

" The child will see the sea, Om Hassan! "

insisted Abou Nawass, his hands cupped round his mouth. " By God, he will go into the sea! "

" Do you hear me, Om Hassan? " continued Okkasionne. " I'm telling you the good news—the child will see the sea! "

A smile appeared on her lips; she heard their voices. Great rivers were flowing. Om Hassan let herself be gently carried along.

The child was everywhere, the child existed; near her, before her, in the voices, in the hearts of these men. He was not dead, he could no longer die. It seemed as though the voices were singing. Between the earth and tomorrow, between the earth and out yonder the song was uninterrupted.

" Life, the sea," she whispered. " At last the sea. . . ."